Simon Ackroyd grew up in Heavy Woollen district of Yorkshire at a time of significant social upheaval due to the closure of the factories and mines in the 1980's. Faced with a bleak future, Simon followed his father's advice and kept the threads of his education intact to gain a degree in science. After a few years working in the industry, he took a job in recruitment that eventually led to a chance meeting – that created a service helping school children find work experience as part of an alternative curriculum. This unexpectedly exposed Simon to the poverty and neglect that lies beneath the surface of some of the more prosperous towns in the county of Yorkshire and inspired him to write this book. Simon lives in the Yorkshire Dales with his wife, three children, dogs, sheep and hens.

I would like to thank Professor Susan Bassnett for her invaluable advice, support and encouragement in helping me completing this book.

Simon Ackroyd

SNOWFLAKE

AUSTIN MACAULEY PUBLISHERS™

Copyright © Simon Ackroyd 2024

The right of Simon Ackroyd to be identified as author of this work has been asserted by the author in accordance with sections 77 and 78 of the Copyright, Designs and Patents Act 1988.

All rights reserved. No part of this publication may be reproduced, stored in a retrieval system, or transmitted in any form or by any means, electronic, mechanical, photocopying, recording, or otherwise, without the prior permission of the publishers.

Any person who commits any unauthorised act in relation to this publication may be liable to criminal prosecution and civil claims for damages.

This is a work of fiction. Names, characters, businesses, places, events, locales, and incidents are either the products of the author's imagination or used in a fictitious manner. Any resemblance to actual persons, living or dead, or actual events is purely coincidental.

A CIP catalogue record for this title is available from the British Library.

ISBN 9781398436664 (Paperback)
ISBN 9781398436671 (ePub e-book)

www.austinmacauley.co.uk

First Published 2024
Austin Macauley Publishers Ltd®
1 Canada Square
Canary Wharf
London
E14 5AA

I would like to acknowledge the tireless dedication of teachers who work in SEND and similar behavioural roles in schools and other educational settings that endeavour to help the most vulnerable students that grow up in the most challenging of circumstances. Without their input many young people would be facing a bleak future.

Money for Nothing

Opening the gate had become the start of many similar but equally differing journeys. My eyes were usually met with the view of an unkempt garden, a path strewn with discarded toys, litter and even clothes blown across the lawn. I would enter with trepidation because there's often dog shit hiding in the long grass, bikes and even furniture blocking the way. On my visit today, there were indeed toys but also piles of pizza boxes and what seemed like endless mounds of empty lager cans, vodka bottles and full-fat cola, a mini recycling centre past its sell-by date. The next-door neighbour watched me from his front window with a steely glare. Anyone with an ID badge was obviously trouble; I had still yet to learn that it's best not to show your ID until you're at the door to avoid attracting unnecessary attention. The thing is, I wasn't there to stand in judgement over the poverty and potential neglect, I was there to try and organise work experience for a 15-year-old teenager, something so basic that it shouldn't cause anyone alarm.

The knock on the door led to the inevitable frantic barking from an unknown beast within. When the door eventually opened after the third knock, the little terror shot out of the house and barked incessantly. The third knock is my key measure. More than three knocks and you're desperate to find someone, a bit like a bailiff. If you knock just once before leaving, it is clear you would rather not have the door answered at all, like when you were a child and you've kicked your ball into a neighbour's garden, a particularly miserable neighbour who will never give it back. Therefore, you knock hoping they won't answer and then you can jump over the fence to retrieve it. Two knocks on the door is still too tentative and non-committal, so three is my rule, forceful enough but not desperate.

"You don't mind dogs, do you?" said the woman behind the door lurking in the gloom of the hallway.

"No, not at all, I like them," I replied without adding that I liked them if they weren't barking like a demented fire alarm. I showed my ID and was ushered into the back room, complete with a grubby toddler, 50-inch TV on full blast and a nosy neighbour. In the corner, watching the TV was Chloe.

"This is Chloe," said the woman.

"Hi, Chloe," I said. "I'm Charlie, I'm here to…"

"I'm going to get a ped when I'm 16," said Chloe, stopping me short.

"A what?" I replied.

"A ped, A MOPED." She sneered, clearly not impressed by my presence. I'd heard this many a time from aspirational teenagers desperate for personal freedom. Unfortunately, most of them discover weed before they discover the big wide world via the two wheels of a 50cc moped. Weed is cheaper and easier to access than alcohol and is more often sold by runners no older than they are. The dreams of a moped would quickly disappear in a cloud of smoke.

"Do you know why I'm here?" I said to the throng, noticing the deep cracks of the worn leather sofa. As I sat down, the cracks opened to reveal a smorgasbord of skanky tapas; a collection of pizza crumbs and fine dust of what I could only assume was poppadom and lost bits of chocolate waiting invitingly for the next insect infestation to come along. I made a mental note to use the hand sanitiser I kept in my glove box when I left. This relationship with hand sanitiser was a familiar one, particularly with Chloe. Personal hygiene was clearly optional and if I had to give a student a lift, which in the case of Chloe turned out to be often, I also had to clean the door handles, seats and anything else she'd touched; a frantic 30-second car valet that made my arms burn.

"Eh?" said Chloe so I repeated myself.

"Oh yeah.... summat about work experience."

Like a woman suddenly blessed with the manners of a royal butler, mum looked disapprovingly at her daughter, almost as if Chloe had only just appeared the night before with all her bad habits; habits that had nothing to do with her. I also noticed I had drawn the attention of the toddler. He scuttled over covered in what looked like jam, oozing from the mangled form of a sandwich he must have been clutching for some time. I prayed that the TV would draw him back as I was struggling to make myself heard.

"Can you turn the TV down please and I'll talk you through the process?" I asked. Over the next 30 minutes, I played along with how Chloe was misunderstood and how she was a good girl really.

Eventually, I managed to establish she had scant interest in school or work, even getting out of bed was a chore and it was plainly a step too far to have a good wash. However, at least I discovered she had an interest in animals, particularly horses and I knew then that it would be easy to place Chloe with Liz, the friendly owner of the nearby riding stables in Manorton.

With a quick look around the room, I made my excuses and stood up moving to the door and as I left the house, I noticed for the first time that there was no hall carpet, just a bare concrete floor and then also a smell that was a common feature of my home visits; the smell of Febreze.

My job may not be familiar to many people but there was and is a growing need for alternatives to the academic curriculum. We had set up our service a few years before in the heart of Yorkshire, helping 15- and 16-year-old teenagers get work experience placements to reduce the time they spend in school and to improve their job prospects. It was becoming a bit of a success because there are hundreds if not thousands of young adults not engaging in school for a variety of reasons, mostly related to poor parenting and weak boundaries from when they were little children. Work experience was proving to be a positive step in creating the good citizens these young people were meant to be.

Within a few days, I had arranged the placement with Liz, who was more than happy to help and so armed with my sanitiser, I collected Chloe from home. Unfortunately, it was clear she wasn't prepared for a visit to a riding stable as she was wearing fashionable but wholly inappropriate sliders or flip-flops as I knew them. She was obviously nervous, so I resisted the temptation to challenge her on her choice of footwear, just in case she refused to go. From bitter experience, I knew there was a realistic prospect of popping her fragile confidence. It was a typical autumn day, with the falling leaves performing a merry dance as we set off in the car and the rain spitting lightly on the windscreen. It was only a couple of miles to the riding school and we quickly had Chloe cooing over horses and wishing idly that she could have a ride there and then. To her obvious shock, it became clear that looking after horses involved a lot of shovelling. Shit mainly, and lots of it and a pair of sliders did not cut the mustard. Can't say I've ever seen a ballerina tip-toeing around a riding school but Chloe made rather a good job of it.

I felt a bit sorry for her at that moment. Her upbringing was not her fault and the lessons she had learnt at home were based on basic survival. However, this was poverty founded on skewed priorities, something that many people have observed, particularly with the growth of social media. It doesn't matter how badly off someone is, they generally have a massive TV, a TV so big it means the sofa may not fit in the living room. I've seen situations where people have simply got rid of the sofa, or put the TV on the floor in front of the fireplace, or even on a bracket so that when the TV is levered away from the wall on that bracket, you can't leave the room because it blocks the doorway. And in almost all cases when I visit people's homes the TV is never, ever switched off.

Also, I had already seen Chloe's total lack of confidence outside of the home and she is not alone. I've observed many teenagers show confidence, if not arrogance in familiar surroundings and then become very wary and tentative once outside. Even the most disruptive children can be reduced to a bag of nerves when meeting new people in unfamiliar surroundings such as a work environment. Often the fear is that these kids will continue to exhibit poor behaviour but I find they tend not to. At home, they may be kings or queens but take them outside of that environment and they become mice. Chloe was a mouse that would need help, so I got to work sorting out her placement. I quickly organised her bus journey there and back which was only 2 stops on one bus. I also sorted her some footwear out of my own pocket. In fact, they were expensive leather yard boots my wife no longer needed that fitted Chloe a treat. All in all, Chloe was set up to fit in nicely at the stables but as I learnt the hard way, it wasn't long before it all began to unravel.

I took Chloe on her first day, full of enthusiasm and interest, talking quickly in short breaths like she'd been running for a bus and had just got on-board before it set off. Our conversation in the car didn't have a lot of time to develop as it wasn't a long journey but I often ask students if they'd had a good evening.

"No!" she replied quickly. "Little nipper got into my room and started messin' with me stuff."

"Pardon?" I replied.

"Yer know, our Nathan got into me room. Up ladder n'all!"

"What do you mean up the ladder?"

"You know," she repeated, "he got up ladder inter loft where me room is. He's only 18-month-old."

I had this vision of a grubby jam-laden kid teetering at the top of a fireman's ladder and she saw my face suddenly widen in disbelief.

"Oh, don't worry, he can climb the ladder alright but when he gets inter loft where me bed is, he can't see what he's doin' because there's no window and he messes up me makeup and clothes while he's staggerin' around."

I quickly gathered my thoughts. "How many people live in your house?" I asked.

"Well, me mam and her boyfriend have one bedroom, then me sisters share the other. They're younger'n me and Nathan sleeps in a cot next to me mam."

"So, you've just got 2 bedrooms?" I offered.

"Yeah, that's why Dave put a ladder inter loft so I could have some privacy."

"Who's Dave?"

"Me mam's boyfriend, he knows a bloke who can get me a 'ped in December when it's me sixteenth birthday."

Clearly, Chloe was moving the subject on but my concerns were growing by the second. My imagination was now running riot. A house crammed with kids, a dog and a 50" TV, with one of the kids trapped in the loft after Dave had set fire to the sofa from a discarded cigarette after falling asleep pissed up on vodka and coke. I would need to contact the school as soon as possible!

I dropped Chloe off and made the call to school. Safeguarding is a key component in keeping young people safe. Wherever we are responsible for them, they have to be safe, at home, at school, at work, everywhere. As part of my job, I make sure students are adequately cared for but there are times when issues at home are a real concern and this was one of them. School it seems was aware of the living arrangements and had contacted the local authority. They paid a visit and said the minimum requirements would be an escape window but couldn't approve the work. However, because they couldn't find alternative accommodation with more bedrooms, they suggested Chloe slept on the sofa. Over the following months, it became clear that Chloe's sleeping arrangements never changed and when she did turn 16, suddenly she began talking about her boyfriend who stayed over every so often. How they all got on in that house I never found out and stopped asking. It was either in hand or being ignored.

I was now nurturing a real sense of sympathy for Chloe. I dropped her off at the riding centre thinking about how easy it is to accept one's situation, normalise it and then try to build a life from it. I tried to place myself in that situation, walking in her shoes. It made me shudder. It's a cycle that we have to break but how do we help those who do not know how to help themselves? At least if a kid doesn't want to do their studies, we can provide alternatives to try and spark their imagination and we offer work experience; community-based work experience with real people, in real businesses. I felt I could make a difference or at least make a good attempt at it. The thing is I feel sorry for some young people. They didn't ask to be born into poverty or neglect. They don't know any better when their parents don't afford them the care they need and I feel a real sense of duty to try and help them improve their lives. It just doesn't come with any guarantees.

But how stupid am I? I was soon knocked off my stride when by the next week I took a call from Chloe's mum.

"Is that Charlie?" She paused and gulped. "Work experience, Charlie? It's Sandra, Chloe's Mam," she spluttered. Toast, I thought, she's eating toast.

"Yes, it is. What's up?" I was learning fast that a call from a school, parent, employer, student, etc, etc was going to be bad news.

"It's our Chloe, she's ere. Said she missed the bus. I took the lad to school at about half eight and when I got back, she was here. Can you come get her and take her to work experience? There in't another bus for two hours."

For God's sake, it's one bus, two stops, how hard can it be? "Yeah, sure. I'll be around in five minutes," I said.

Sure enough, five minutes later I was waiting outside but to my surprise, Chloe wasn't waiting for me. I sat in the car with the engine running for a little while until frustrated, I eventually got out of the car and walked through the gate. Before I had even knocked on the door, the alarm dog was going off like the clappers. The door slowly opened and Chloe appeared almost nonchalantly with a made-up face that looked like it had been rubbed with a rag. She didn't say a word, just left the door open so that the rat dog could bounce in and out.

"I'll wait by the car," I said.

About 2 minutes later, she reappeared. "Can I have a fag before we go?" she asked.

"If you insist, we're already late," I replied with frustration and jumped in the car. I read some emails on my smartphone, started the engine and eventually, she slid into the passenger seat in a huff. I didn't ask what was on her mind; however, I got to find out even though it wasn't something I wanted to hear.

"Last night, I went out wi' me mates and called Dave to pick me up at about half ten," she muttered angrily. "Well, fuckin' car wunt start, would it? Had to walk all way the home on me own."

"Oh right, sounds like a pain. What time did you get home?" I asked, completely disinterested.

"About midnight. Didn't get to bed till one, 'cause Dave was pissed off that I was so late, he was rantin' and ravin'. Said I shouldn't rely on lifts to get home on time."

"Can you not swear please," I replied.

"Sorry but Dave can be a right arsehole. Dunt like me hangin' out in town. I reckon his car wasn't even broken so he could have a go at me."

We continued the journey in relative silence and arrived half an hour late. I apologised to Liz, the owner of the riding school. Chloe just ambled off to the staff room to get changed.

I didn't think any more about Chloe until the next time she was due for work experience and again her mother called with a similar tale.

"Chloe reckons bus just drove straight past her; she was here when I got back. Can you get her again?"

"What do you mean drove straight past?" I said in disbelief.

"Aye, it's what she said. Drove straight past. Full apparently," she replied. "Can you come 'cause I've got to get Nathan to the doctors; he's got a sniff."

I went to pick up Chloe once more who was wearing the same clothes as last time with that faint but familiar smell of Febreze wafting in the back-ground.

So, what is it about Febreze? I used to quite like the smell until I worked out what it was used for. The adverts for air fresheners portray the image of a country home with wide-open windows and bright airy rooms dappled with sunlight and a well-to-do housewife wafting around the house spraying everything. In some of the homes I visit however, it's the opposite; houses untouched for months with dirty plates strewn across the kitchen worktops, piles of clothes and shoes, food bits on the carpet and furniture, and grubby handprints on walls. The fact is that people use Febreze instead of washing clothes, instead of hoovering, instead of changing the bed or polishing the furniture. In one advert you can clearly see a woman spraying a beautifully made-up bed with air freshener, a green light for some of the parents I visit to spray with gusto, usually just as I arrive. It shouldn't be a surprise to know that I gag slightly whenever I smell it or see a can of it on the TV stand.

On that morning, it had been raining quite heavily and I was a bit surprised that the smell of air freshener wasn't rising like a miasma in a tropical swamp off Chloe's damp, warm clothes. The thing was that she didn't have so much as a drop of water anywhere on her clothes or hair? How could that be if she had walked to the bus stop and back in the pouring rain?

I didn't really think too much about it, I just set off for the riding school.

"Have you got any lunch?" I asked. I could see she didn't have a bag with her and was wearing trainers. It was another one of those questions to see whether the student was looking after themselves but the trainers were new.

"Na," she replied. "I'm not 'ungry."

"I think you might be hungry later, why don't we go to the supermarket on the way and get a sandwich or something," I replied. I could see she was getting twitchy with my insistence.

"Na, you're alright," she said hastily. "I'll get summat off a mate if I need to."

"I can pay if you like," I offered.

"No ta, I'm just not bothered," she said with finality.

Faced with her resoluteness, I backed down and dropped her off, sweeping the stains off the car seats with sanitiser when she'd left.

Chloe wandered off to the tea room in her new trainers.

However, something was niggling me. Call me thick but I've usually got 20 or so kids at any one time and any one of them can throw a bomb into my day and ruin it by not turning up, walking off, or just being a little arse but with Chloe, something wasn't ringing true. With that in mind, the next week I made up my mind to make sure the bus was running OK to at least eliminate that as the problem. Giving myself 10 minutes to spare, I parked the car at a discreet distance from the bus stop so as not to be seen and waited. Sure enough, a half-empty bus arrived on time and a couple of people got off but no Chloe. So where was she? The phone didn't ring to say she had walked back home so I was starting to get worried. I rang mum with no answer. I drove to the house. Even the dog alarm didn't bring anyone to the door, even after 5 knocks! I rang the school to explain and they said I should wait until mum got back from the school run.

It was about 11:30 am when the phone rang. It was school.

"Hi, it's Janet from attendance," she continued. "I've spoken to Chloe's mum and basically according to Chloe, she did get on the bus. However, the bus didn't stop at the riding centre but carried on, over the ring road and eventually pulled over at the stop in Templethwaite village where she got off. She didn't have any money so she had to walk back and had only just got home. This isn't really acceptable as she's a vulnerable girl."

Vulnerable girl my arse, I'm being played here, I thought. However, with significant restraint, I replied, "I don't know what's going on but I do know what did happen. I waited near the bus stop this morning to make sure the service was running normally and it came on time. It also stopped and let a couple of passengers off. Therefore, either Chloe didn't get on the bus or she forgot to get off."

"That's interesting," she said. "However, there's something else. Because you've been picking her up, her mum says that you insisted on taking her bus money to pay for the petrol." She paused for effect. I sat there seething. "She says that when she had asked for Chloe's bus money back, Chloe didn't have it because you took it. Is that true?"

Is that true? The lying little toe rag. I did however have an ace up my sleeve that could put all this uncertainty to bed.

"Janet," I said with the confidence and smoothness of a darting dolphin, "I have a dashcam in my car that constantly records the road and fortunately, every conversation that takes place in the vehicle. I can reassure you and in fact prove that I never would ask for petrol money and in this case, never did."

"I thought that would be the situation," she replied. "I believe that when confronted with the truth, Chloe will deny everything, become aggressive, and therefore, be excluded from school for a few days to calm down." My dashcam has proven to be a saviour on many occasions, it cost £40 and can literally put paid to any student shenanigans as it did here.

Over the next few days, I liaised with the school and it was decided that due to Chloe's deceitfulness, she would be removed from the work experience program. I didn't think about Chloe again until I visited a second-hand market in town. There she was, walking towards me with one of her mates. We exchanged pleasantries, with her telling me that she'd got a job as a cleaner and was loving it and that she was hoping to buy a moped in the summer. Even though she had turned 16, it was too cold to ride a bike around. The irony wasn't lost on me regarding the cleaning job. I winced at the thought of bed-clothes not being changed and instead, treated by the liberal application of Febreze. However, as I was walking along, something caught my eye on one of the stalls. I wandered over to have a look and sure enough, there sat on the stall in pride of place amongst the tat and rubbish was a pair of expensive yard boots. Yard boots I was sure that I had given to Chloe and had belonged to my wife.

"Where did you get these from?" I asked the stall holder.

Although she looked a bit taken aback by my request, she replied, "You see that girl walking away over there? The one you were chatting to? I buy things off her from time to time. She sold me these about 4 months ago. In fact, I've just bought a riding hat off her."

"4 months ago?" I exclaimed. That was when she had just started work experience. "How much did you pay her?"

"£50, I think. She said she didn't need them anymore, said she wanted new trainers and some cigarettes from a mate who had loads to get rid of and they were going cheap."

The sneaky little swine. The devious, thieving bugger! Pocketing her bus money, probably pocketing her lunch money and pinching riding hats and now selling my boots! She probably did work experience in her sliders or her new trainers. More likely she just sat in the tea-room.

"Can I buy them from you?" I said quickly. "I'll give you what you paid for them. You've had them a while so obviously, they're not selling."

"Are you having a laugh?" she replied. "These are quality. They cost £250 brand new."

Tell me about it, I thought. I know I paid for them as a Christmas present!

"I tell you what," she continued, "you can have them for £100."

As the gall rose to burn my tonsils, I politely refused her offer. I'd been had, done up like a kipper and I just couldn't bring myself to buy them back.

Non-Fiction Factory

The phone tends to ring when you least want or expect it to. It was 7:30 am when the shrill, increasingly urgent sound of my phone started to grow. Oh God, it's starting already.

"Hi, is that Charlie from the Work Scheme?" A very bubbly voice chirped.

"Speaking," I replied, rather more enthusiastically than I meant, slowly putting down my coffee cup.

"Oh brilliant!" She exclaimed. "We've had a recommendation from Barnton Grammar School that you were doing excellent work with their students and we would like to refer a nice young man who could do with some help."

In a conversation such as this, I feel the pressing need to interpret what the teacher is really thinking at that moment. It also helps me to readjust my thoughts to ensure I understand the real motive behind the phone call which might be;

"Please help me, I've tried everything to engage with this student but he is ignoring everything we say and we are at the end of our tether."

Regardless of the reality gap, I understand why teachers have such a bright outlook when they ring us. That's because they are relieved that someone can possibly help them. In our rural county, there's very little alternative provision available to schools and therefore, teachers have to be resourceful and try to find solutions themselves. For the uninitiated, alternative provision means engaging in activities that sit outside the normal academic curriculum. In my case, I offer a work-based alternative that relies on community involvement. However, due to the distance students have to travel to school and the fact that there are relatively few urban areas, even providing services in the towns can have its limitations. This is why The Work Scheme has proven so popular.

I am always conscious that some teachers will brush over the facts when it comes to describing the students' faults. They can be described as misunderstood or simply disruptive, when in fact they are absolute shits, which is why I like to visit schools before I meet students. What made matters worse, in this case, was that there was a real sense of urgency in her voice which put me on my guard right from the start.

Without taking another breath, she continued, "We could really do with you coming in this morning to meet with him if that's possible. Mrs Salbanio at Barnton told me you were so responsive. He's taking his lessons in the behaviour unit so if you can make it you'll need to ask for Mrs Brownlee." She emphasised the 'so responsive' like a professional sycophant.

The behaviour unit is a facility within the school that is used to teach the most difficult and disengaged students. Often the students are aggressive, non-cooperative and don't want to be in school at all. At least if they are in the behaviour unit, they are not a distraction to others in normal lessons and can get more one-on-one tuition. However, being put in the behaviour unit also offered an indication as to the type of young man that was being proposed.

At this point, I still hadn't said anything in response and whoever was on the line wasn't going to let me speak yet. She was like a rabid boxer landing her punches, keeping me on the ropes.

"I'm afraid I won't be available," she continued. "But I look forward to meeting you sometime in the future. Apologies for not introducing myself properly, by the way, my name's Mrs Hardcastle," she said breathlessly.

"Oh hi," I replied. Clearly, she'd made her mind up that I would attend that day. "Can I ask which school you are at and also the student's name? And do you have a time in mind, as I need to check my diary?"

This was an attempt to ring the bell to allow me enough time to gather my thoughts. I could hear her breath catch in her throat almost imperceptibly, and I could sense she was worried I might refuse to take on the student.

Ding, ding! She continued with renewed enthusiasm before I had time to think. "I'm Deputy Head of Lidsdale Community Academy and the student's name is Tyler Dunston. I'm sure you'll get on really well with him, he just needs to be among adults rather than other kids, that's why we think work experience would be really good for him."

She chatted on without checking in an attempt to pin me down, and then wham! "Is your diary free for 10 am?"

Knock-down! I was free at that time.

But the truth is that I would have made time anyway as I just can't say no and never have. It's not about the money and though this might come as a bit of a shock, I actually care about the kids. I slowly got up off the metaphorical canvas, the blows having lined my face with concern, hoping to God her expectations weren't too high.

"Yes, I'm sure I can make that time," I said, looking for solace in my coffee cup.

"Oh that's fantastic," she purred, removing her gloves.

Some teachers really are as hard as nails!

I arrived at the school later that morning, and to some surprise, I found that everyone I met from reception to the behaviour unit were well-briefed and expecting me so I was soon sitting with Mrs Brownlee in her small office on the south side of the building. It had a single tiny window and a huge radiator, emitting waves of heat like the sands of a hot desert.

"A couple of things you need to know about Tyler," she said in her introduction. "Firstly, he's very wary of people he doesn't know." Brilliant!

"Secondly, he has a personal hygiene problem."

I blanched, hoping he didn't smell of Febreze.

"It can be pretty bad," she continued. "So we've had a shower fitted in the boy's toilets so he can freshen up if it has become overwhelming. It smells…" – she paused somewhat embarrassed and then lowered her voice – "…a bit like cheese that's going off.

"However, you're lucky today as he's had a shower and is wearing the spare uniform we keep just in case. Let's just see how you get on with him. If it's OK with you, I'll sit in on the meeting to reassure him, so if you can hang on for 5 minutes I'll just go and get him."

I nodded in agreement. I wasn't sure whether to laugh or cry.

It does however demonstrate the lengths some schools will go to, to help students with both their academic requirements and their social and emotional needs. The level of support can be phenomenal, including early intervention workers, mental health practitioners, extra tuition, youth justice intervention or special educational intervention that includes services like The Work Program. Whether Tyler was aware of this or even cared, was to be discovered.

Just then the door inched open slowly and in walked the living dead; 6ft tall, 4ft wide with a completely blank expression, quickly followed by Mrs Brownlee who had suddenly suffered a remarkable change of personality. No longer straight-talking and honest but crooning and patronising.

"Here we are, Tyler," she sang. "Sir is going to help you find work experience, aren't you, sir?"

Tyler's eyes never moved from the floor.

"You sit down there, Tyler, and we can have a little chat about it. Nothing to worry about."

Tyler shuffled into the nearest chair, his eyes glued to the ubiquitous patterned carpet. He didn't say a word. He looked like a pet bear.

"Now then, sir, would you like to explain to Tyler what you do and how it will work?"

Having been knocked about by the deputy head earlier that morning, I was now being thrown into the deep end with my hands tied behind my back by the head of the behavioural unit. It was like dealing with Al Capone's mob.

"Hi, Tyler!" I cleared my throat. "My name is Charlie and school has asked me to help you find work experience to help with your studies."

No reply.

"If it's OK with you, I would like to ask some simple questions to help discover what you might like to do. Is that OK?"

Silence.

"So what are you interested in?" I said and tried a smile.

The silence in the room continued. Mrs Brownlee just sat by with a false-looking grin on her lips that spread wider as I continued smiling.

"School says you're interested in work experience, Tyler, and I'm here to help," I said again. I had even dropped my tone of voice to add gravity. I felt a bit like one of those patronising politicians as they address the nation with bad news.

Nothing.

Now I was starting to feel the heat in the room as a trickle of sweat ran down my ribs and onto the waistband of my jeans.

I gave in to the silence. "Tyler," I said starting to feel exasperated, "if only you could let me know what you think."

No response. I seemed to be drowning in perspiration. Mrs Brownlee watched on, ignoring the fact that I was turning redder by the minute.

I tried a new tack. "OK then, let me start by asking what you like about the school?"

Silence.

"How would describe your behaviour in school?"

Deathly silence now.

"OK, what would you like to do for work experience?"

A slight shuffle, his eyes darting in my direction. Then he closed them firmly.

"What are you interested in?" I said desperately, casting a longing look at the window wishing it would open to allow cool, sweet air to flow into the room.

A shrug and then, "Dunno," he said. At last, he had spoken! But I was getting the bare minimum.

"OK," I replied and shot a glance at Mrs Brownlee who was willing Tyler to talk, her gaze so intense that surely even Tyler must be feeling the heat. I felt the life belt slip over my shoulders when she spoke.

"Come on, Tyler, it's nothing to be worried about, just tell sir what you might like to do."

The lifebelt wasn't feeling too secure. This lad was being uncooperative because he didn't want to do anything. His size, hygiene and demeanour told me that he wanted to be left alone to watch TV all day and eat. I couldn't help feeling the school's approach was doing Tyler no favours at all.

Tyler didn't give a shit.

"Dunno," he said.

"Maybe this is a bit overwhelming," I offered. "Would it be better if we tried meeting again with your mum around? Would that be possible, Mrs Brownlee?"

"That's a great idea!" she replied a bit too enthusiastically. "What do you think of that, Tyler?" She almost sang. "Do you think mum being involved would help?"

"S'pose," he mumbled. His eyes were still firmly closed like he was in hibernation. "Can I go now?" he said, and before Mrs Brownlee could respond, he slowly stood up, filling the small room with his bulk. Without a further word, he shuffled to the door, opened it and went out. I assumed he'd opened his eyes because he was too ungainly to achieve that feat with them shut.

"Take him for something to eat," offered Mrs Brownlee. "He always responds well to food." With that, she offered her goodbyes, remembering to give me Tyler's mum's contact details and with a sigh of resignation I left, my shirt stuck to my ribs wondering whether I'd met a student or the largest school pet I'd ever seen.

Having organised to meet again a few days later, I found myself standing outside Tyler's front door. Negotiating the garden path had been relatively easy, just an old sock plastered to the cold flags and a large pile of cigarette ends beneath the living room window. These were the only signs of neglect I could see. I rang the bell and the door was quickly answered by Tyler's mum.

"Hi, I'm Charlie," I said. "I'm here to discuss Tyler's work experience."

"Oh hello," she replied. "I'm Tracey and we've been expecting you, we're in the front room." I stepped into the hallway and then over a large roll of linoleum to get into the living room. The floor, walls and stairwell were completely bare.

Tyler was in the living room which was piled high with clothes, furniture and other items that would normally be spread throughout the house. He was watching an enormous TV, laughing and giggling to himself, completely ignoring my presence. The sofa he was on was one of two sitting opposite each other with the TV in the window between them, creating a gloom that was punctuated by the flickering screen. The best way to watch the TV was to lie on the sofa, head on the armrest looking straight ahead. That was where Tyler was. In his own little world.

Having taken in this visual feast, I was then confronted by the smell; a cloying, sticky odour that stuck in my throat and made me gag. Slowly as my eyes adjusted to the gloom, I could see that Tyler's clothes were encrusted with the remnants of past meals of indeterminate content that if tested forensically, would hint at meals taken weeks ago.

"Sit up, Tyler sweetie," cooed mum.

"Eh?" he replied.

"Sit up," she repeated. "Charlie's here about work experience."

He slowly shuffled his bulk into an upright position. Only then did I see that he was lying on a sleeping bag and his head had been resting on a pillow. I moved to the sofa opposite and noticed that at one end there was another sleeping bag rolled up along with a second pillow.

"He loves watching TV, don't you, T? Can you turn it down though, love?" she asked politely. With a grunt, Tyler turned down the sound and then giggled to himself.

"What's funny, Tyler?" I asked.

"Nowt," he said.

"Oh OK. Well if you want, we can go through some of the questions I didn't get a chance to ask the other day," I replied. He just shrugged his shoulders.

"Let's start with your hobbies. What do you like to do?" Again I was met with silence but this time mum stepped in.

"Like I said, he loves watching TV, particularly Disney films. He collects the DVDs for birthdays and Christmas, don't you, T?"

I looked on incredulously at this large 16-year-old school pet. I would have expected him to be out with his friends getting up to no good but this young man was hiding away from life not engaging in school, not engaging with me and not engaging with the broader world and he was a Disney fanatic. His life was simply watching TV, eating his meals in front of the TV and more than likely, sleeping in front of it with his mum sleeping on the other sofa; a bizarre state of affairs.

The rest of the interview followed the same pattern, a shrug of the shoulders and then mum interjecting with answers. I soon learnt that Tyler had never been on a bus on his own and had never been into town without his mum. He wouldn't even buy anything from a shop. I had this image of his mum pushing Tyler around in a huge buggy, puffing and panting as she shoved him up the hills and clinging on for dear life as they descended the other side. How the hell was I going to get Tyler out from under his mum's wing and into work experience? And if I did, how likely was it that he would turn up?

The only option I had was to do a few weeks of life skills lessons on a one-to-one basis. Not the ideal answer but the school was desperate for me to remain involved with him. The plan would be to get him work experience in a charity shop and build up to that by getting him on a bus, showing him how to buy a ticket and getting him to go into town to the shop I had identified as a potential employer.

With that in mind, we began to meet in town at McDonalds. Firstly, this meant I didn't have to go back to the house and secondly, I could at least get Tyler more active. I would buy him lunch while his mum went shopping and we would go through skills learning.

It was torturous. He never veered from his standard behaviour, shrugging constantly, offering one-word answers, just silently grazing on the food I'd bought for him. Over the coming weeks, my frustration rose with the lack of progress until I declared he was ready for work experience and organised a start date. I was taking a big risk but I believed that Tyler was a very calculating young man. His choice to just coast through life didn't sit very well with me but I had no idea why he was so unmotivated. That was an enigma to me, so I took the decision to provoke some sort of response from the bear.

When I told Tyler of my plans, he had a look of utter fear on his face. He even stopped chewing for a brief moment.

"I need to speak to mum," he said. And that's all he said. He finished his meal and sat staring out of the window. I took my phone out of my pocket and rang his mum and told her of my plans and Tyler's subsequent reaction. We agreed to meet in the department store along the street on the lower ground floor where the children's clothes were.

As I entered the store, I searched for the stairs and escalator and took the escalator down to the lower ground. Sure enough, I found her near the cashier's desk but when I turned around, Tyler was nowhere to be seen. Panic quickly set in. Under normal circumstances, a 16-year-old could negotiate their way through town without help but in this case, I was responsible for Tyler and he wasn't a normal everyday 16-year-old.

"Where's Tyler?" she said.

"I don't know, he was there right behind me no more than 30 seconds ago," I replied in panic. Then without any drama, she responded knowingly.

"I know what it is," she said. "He's scared of escalators."
"Pardon?" I said.

"He's scared of escalators. He won't go on them; he'll be standing at the top all on his own, dithering. Don't worry, he won't actually move, he'll just wait there until you or I go to fetch him."

By now my patience for Tyler and his foibles was wearing thin. As mum had suggested, Tyler was indeed standing at the top of the escalator, head down swaying slightly.

"Hi, T. What's up," she said.

"Don't want to," he blurted.

"Don't want to what?" she said. "Use the escalator? You don't have to, you know, the stairs are over there," she replied pointing to a green exit sign.

"Not that," he barked. "Work experience!"

"You'll enjoy it, I know you will."

"Don't want to."

She then turned to me and shrugged. "You can try and take him but if T doesn't want to do something, he won't do it."

I could easily appreciate that, he was verging on 20 stone! I couldn't see anyone forcing him to move if he didn't want to. However, I was determined to get this young man out into the real world, so a few days later and regardless of his protestations, I picked him up in my car at the allotted time and dropped him off at the shop. He shuffled inside and the well-meaning manager took him into the back warehouse to sort out donated clothes and toys. When I returned to the car, I gave it a liberal clean to rid it of the cheesy smell.

Later that day, I went back to the shop to collect him, only to find he wasn't there.

I could have killed him, walking out on a good placement, letting down an employer who was unlikely to take another student.

Where the hell is he?

I quickly found the manager.

"Oh no, he didn't walk out. He took a phone call about 11:30 am and then the police came to get him at about 1 o'clock," she said reassuringly but I was confused.

"The police? What has he done?" I asked.

"I don't think he's done anything wrong and they didn't really say anything, they just asked him to go with them. Shame really as he was doing really well and he seemed to be enjoying it."

"Wow, OK," I said. "I'll try and find out what's happened and will let you know as soon as I can." And with that, I left.

As soon as I could, I rang the school to let Mrs Brownlee know what had happened. She had no idea herself but promised to let me know as soon as she could. Two weeks went by and I still hadn't heard anything. I even went to the charity shop because they were concerned about him. It was comforting to think that they cared. I had also received no response at all from his mum, no matter how many times I rang her. The lack of news about Tyler was worrying, so in the end, I rang the school again. The phone rang out for quite a while but eventually, Mrs Brownlee answered with a hint of exasperation.

"Oh sorry," she said after I had explained the reasons for my call. "In all the confusion, I completely forgot to ring you." She continued, "It really is a sorry affair, Tyler is now living with his grandma in Sheffield for the foreseeable future so we won't be needing work experience anymore, thank you."

I got the impression she wasn't being particularly helpful which was confusing as I had done as much as I could to help Tyler, so I wasn't going to let this go so lightly. After all, I had responded quickly to their request to meet Tyler, seen through all his issues to work with him and in the end, I had found him a placement which was only scuppered because he had been mysteriously taken away by the police.

"OK," I replied, "but what happened?"

"Well," she continued somewhat reluctantly, "the police arrested his mum for running a cannabis plant factory in the bedrooms of the house. The police helicopter spotted it on their infra-red camera. Apparently, the family were living in the front room. The rest of the house was used to grow the plants and handle distribution."

Shock doesn't do justice to describe the feelings I had at that moment. Tyler and his mum were heavily involved in drug dealing? The signs had been there, particularly the sleeping arrangements but I hadn't put two and two together because I had been so distracted by Tyler's demeanour! I got the impression the school felt I had missed a trick with Tyler, although in my mind, they were just as culpable in not spotting the signs. It was acutely embarrassing, so I simply thanked her for the information and said goodbye.

On reflection, however, there was one crumb of comfort to be taken from the situation. I could at least conclude that Tyler was actually motivated by something other than TV dinners. If only I had known he was interested in horticulture, it would have made finding a work experience placement much, much easier.

Nothing But a Dreamer

My eyes slowly eased open at the prompt of the sun's rays cutting through the zipped entrance. The first thing I saw was the cotton netting of the tent, sagging slightly as the bell-shaped shelter had settled overnight. Beside me, Lauren's breathing was still rhythmic with sleep but as I adjusted myself, the air bed responded like a bucking bronco and she began to rise on the moving tide of air before gently falling back again, prompting a flickering of her eyes as she started to wake. As she recognised my face, a smile passed across it but was swiftly replaced by a blank stare.

I opened the tent to a bright blue morning; we were in the middle of France on a holiday quickly organised due to my recent redundancy. An opportunity for us to think about what I could do next.

"Tea?" I asked Lauren. She ignored me. I filled the kettle to the brim and put it on the weak flame of the burner.

She sat up slightly and settled herself onto her forearm.

"Tea?" I repeated.

"Yes," she replied. I was a little taken aback. She'd been a bit quiet on the way down to France but that seemed to be developing into a frost, in stark contrast to the warmth of the morning air.

"What's up, Lauren?" I asked. She sighed slightly and laid back down again under the covers.

"What are we going to do?" she said, staring at the roof of the tent, ignoring my question.

The urge to answer honestly and admit I didn't have a clue was strong but was quickly suppressed by a need to gain more time to gather my thoughts. I didn't reply immediately, I just fiddled about with the brimming kettle. I didn't want to rush my answer.

"I'll think of something," I replied but it didn't sound very convincing. It was clear that after 8 years of marriage, I needed to up my game and offer Lauren the reassurance she needed.

"I hope you can because it's a lot to sacrifice," she said. She paused, and then went on. "The thing is, Charlie, I just don't understand why you didn't tell me."

"Things moved so quickly," I replied. "The company was looking at making wholesale changes and I didn't feature as part of their future plans. It was pointless trying to fight them."

I drifted off a little thinking about the events of the past few weeks. Friends who I thought were friends, turned out not to be. 10 years of hard graft had been discarded. 10 years of commitment bought out for 30 pieces of redundancy silver. I had to admit I felt a little betrayed.

I was quickly brought back to reality by Lauren repeating the same question. "Why didn't you tell me, Charlie, I might have been able to help," she said.

"Because I was faced with a simple decision," I replied. "Either pretend I supported the new plans for the business or say what I really felt."

Lauren glanced at me with a knowing look. My honesty was an asset but equally could lead to trouble.

"The thing is," I continued, "I couldn't compromise my feelings. Things were becoming cut-throat and I didn't have the ability to keep my thoughts inside."

"I'm glad you've shaved off that silly beard," she said with the hint of a smile. The beard had been part of the metrosexual uniform which came with the job, along with the pin-striped suit and the cufflinks. It all had to go.

I laughed. It was the first glimmer that Lauren would get over what had happened and was defrosting slightly. I climbed onto the air bed again to wait for the kettle to boil causing another tidal wave of air that made us wallow on its surface. The tiny burner had been valiantly attempting to heat the kettle and it must have taken 20 minutes to boil. That gave me plenty of time to think.

When it slowly began to whistle, Lauren rolled off the air bed to make the tea, leaving me bobbing about once more like flotsam in the sea. Although she was upset with me, her desire to look after me was still a huge driving force. That kind of loving support gives a man confidence that he's not going to be abandoned in his hour of need.

Hiding that reassuring thought, I considered that with any luck, she might forget to be angry anymore and make me a bacon sandwich as well.

Things were starting to look up.

Lauren and I made plans while we were on that holiday and when we talked properly after a cup of tea and a bacon butty, we had agreed on what to do with some of the redundancy money. She would use some of it to set up her own business, which would ultimately become a successful dog kennelling and training centre and we agreed to focus our attention on that to help with our lack of regular income. I would do all the construction work, source and fit the kennels and Lauren would work with clients to train their badly-behaved dogs, something she'd done on and off for years. We gave ourselves 3 months to get things up and running. It was an exciting time.

Our biggest priority was to find appropriate shelters for the dogs and having searched the internet, we found 2 bespoke timber professional dog kennels on an auction site. They were second-hand and well-priced so I put in my bid and waited for the auction to complete. We were chuffed to bits to discover we had won but then we had the task of collecting them from Merseyside, about 2 hour drive away over the Pennines. We hired a van and asked my brother Hayden to help us bring them home.

On arrival at the address, we began wondering whether we had done the right thing. We were parked in a square of garages at the back of a row of council houses. There were old prams and other similarly discarded items, remains of bonfires, piles of paper and bits of cars scattered about. Eventually, an old wooden gate was pushed aside to reveal a man about 30 years old, armed with a jet-wash in one hand and a Staffordshire bull terrier on a short chain in the other.

"Yous come about the kennels, mate?" he said in a drawly scouse accent.

"Yes, the name's, Charlie. Are you Paul?"

"Aye mate. Yous can just wait 5 minutes while I get rid of this dog and I'll sort yous out."

He disappeared back through the gate and reappeared again without the dog. We looked at each other wondering what was coming next.

"I've just put her inside," he said, holding onto his vowels for dear life. "She's not great with strangers."

With that, he fired up the jet wash and beckoned us into the garden. What we found were 2 wooden kennels approximately 15 feet square, made up of 3 cells with an indoor section and outdoor run. As we looked more closely, we could see that each one was covered from top to bottom in dog shit.

"Why are you selling them?" I yelled to overcome the howl of the electric motor of the jet-wash.

"Used to breed Staffordshires," he replied, "but the neighbours called the bizzies because of the noise, so I've got t'sell 'em. They said I needed a licence but that was too expensive."

He continued to play the jet of water back and forth across the flanks of the kennels hopelessly trying to clean the detritus away. The sides, back, the bars, the locks, the doors, everything was covered in a reddy brown smear. There was dog shit everywhere. We looked at each other again and went to sit in the van.

"Charlie," said my brother Hayden, "have you seen the state of those kennels?"

I looked back across to Paul who was doggedly continuing to clean the sides of one of them. However, as I looked again, it was just possible to see that he was revealing a sound structure underneath.

"It looks like they may be OK," I said pointing at Paul who was now splattered in faeces.

"Unlike him," said Hayden. We laughed.

Paul scowled at us while we watched from the van. It was taking so long that I stepped back out of the vehicle and told Paul we were off for lunch and would be back in an hour. When we returned, the kennels were much cleaner and Paul, now soaking wet in slurry, was sitting in a plastic patio chair smoking a cigarette. The dog was back by his side like a menacing bouncer.

"That's a grand for each mate, cash," he drawled.

"We'll pay £850," Hayden responded, taking control over the deal.

"The dog says a grand!" he replied, pulling on the dog chain. It growled while drops of brown-coloured water were dripping off the end of Paul's nose.

"The advert said a grand and they were meant to be dismantled," Hayden pointed out. "These kennels are still in one piece, so we'll pay £850."

"Yous Yorkshires are tight as cramp!" he declared. He looked at his feet and sat thinking for a while, all the time yanking on the dog's chain. "Alright. Done!" he said finally. Hayden flashed a smile and a wink but refused to shake the guy's hand. I handed over the cash with £300 left in my pocket that I didn't expect to have and we set about taking the kennels apart. Luckily, it took less time than we anticipated and we also had the foresight to buy rubber gloves while we were out at lunch to avoid being contaminated as we dismantled the structure. However, as we took things apart, we uncovered hidden corners of shit Paul had missed with the jet-wash and therefore, we were as filthy as Paul had become by the time we'd finished. I'd never felt as desperate for a wash in all my life as I did then and we had a 2 hour drive home still to come. But we worked doggedly for another 20 minutes or so until the panels were in the van and we set off home cursing Paul for being such a filthy scally. I would imagine his neighbours were over the moon to see the kennels gone, although the river of slurry now pooling in the square in front of the garages would be a different problem for them to work out with him.

Over the next week or so, we titivated, painted and renewed the kennel blocks until they were the kind of home even people might sleep in, although there were still a few stubborn reddy brown stains here and there. Our next plan was to email as many people as we could think of about our new venture and it was from one of these emails that we had a response from an old work colleague called Rebecca.

Rebecca explained that she and her husband were intending to visit her family who lived in Scotland and wanted to leave their dog Deefer with someone they knew. She explained that they had never put Deefer in kennels before so didn't know how he would behave, so she asked if it would be OK for them to visit us to make sure Deefer didn't get too stressed locked up behind bars and also make sure the kennels matched their expectations. Lauren and I now had an incentive to get everything as good as it could be, heating, lighting and a separate concrete run for the dogs to socialise in; a proper doggy home from home. Our new venture was now open for business and with Paul's advice ringing in our ears, we made sure the kennels were licensed before Rebecca and her husband visited us.

Rebecca and her husband Ibra, as well as Deefer came to see us a few days later. We exchanged pleasantries and gave them a tour of our brand new premises. They were happy with what they discovered and we were happy to be taking on one of our first clients. It was agreed that Deefer would be staying for a week while they went on to Scotland. So having agreed on a plan and leaving Deefer in his kennel to make sure he was happy, we went for lunch together at our local pub to catch up and reminisce.

"Deefer," I said to Ibra to try and break the ice. "Original." Ibrahim just looked at me with eyes like dark pools, giving no emotion away. Rebecca laughed on his behalf.

"Ignore him," she said. "He's fed up with his job, or more accurately, fed up with his boss. We're off to Scotland to try and calm him down and recharge his batteries."

She talked about him like he wasn't there.

"Alright, Rebecca," said Ibra as he suddenly sprang into life, "you don't know what it's like working for a council that's running out of money and you're faced with a rising number of kids going off the rails."

"What do you do for a job?" asked Lauren.

"He works in youth intervention," replied Rebecca.

"Actually," said Ibra raising one big, bushy eyebrow, "it's a specialist intervention whereby we put young kids in work experience instead of full-time school. Unfortunately, the council can't afford it. They also don't have the employers who can help the students and a policy of wrapping everything in red tape to the point where it won't work anyway. I can see how to untie it all but my boss has a bigger priority in protecting his retirement plan. For that reason alone, he won't rock the boat."

"What are the kids like?" asked Lauren.

Warming to his subject, he responded, "Varied. They're into drugs, crime, and they're disengaged from school.

They're from looked-after backgrounds." Lauren looked puzzled and Ibrahim noticed, so explained. "They're sometimes in foster care, often in poverty, some are even from well-off families. Lots of backgrounds but it's a way of helping them build their self-esteem because they often feel like failures. Unfortunately, the council just don't see the benefits." He paused for breath. "The schools do because they benefit from a lot less disruption. Also, the families benefit because their child is suddenly engaged and interested in life and the community benefits because there's less crime. It's a no-brainer."

"Sounds amazing," replied Lauren as the meals arrived.

As we tackled our food, I found I had a whole raft of questions queuing up in my head. What if a private service could be set up to help those children? Would the schools pay for such a service? Could you find employers willing to give them a chance? What had Ibrahim had to do to make it work? The answers came back quick fire in between mouthfuls of food. Each answer made me grow in confidence about an idea that was forming in my head. Could we set up a business to support these young people and would Ibrahim come in with me to set it up? As the cutlery clattered onto the plates, we settled back in our seats and I asked him the big question.

"Yes," he said quite simply. "As you've probably guessed, I'm really fed up with my current job and I've been looking around for a while but nothing's really come up that I like." He sat back in his chair pondering what to say next. We didn't have to wait long.

"Rebecca's told me a lot about you; how much you care for your colleagues, sorry ex-colleagues!" We laughed.

"How hard you work, how you value honesty, your sense of humour and your ability to communicate with people. I feel like I already know you. So yes, I'll do it."

I was elated. He seemed to be an easy-going man and I was sure he was someone you could trust. All I needed now was some time to get things in place and another new venture would be born. My career in youth intervention was about to begin and I was crapping myself. As time would tell, I was right to be nervous.

Old Macdonald Had a Farm

Keiron Metcalfe sat chuckling at Dan Carter's joke. He was sitting with a can of lager on the banks of the Dowderdale River, which flowed with a gentle meandering grace over shallow reeds and boulders where the boys were night fishing. Poaching to be exact, as neither of them had a fishing licence with the Dowderthwaite angling club. At their feet were numerous empty cans of lager and scattered around them were various cigarette ends, empty crisp packets and the odd spliff. By now it was dark and nearly midnight and the fish had shown no tendency to bite. The boys were starting to get bored.

At 15, neither of them should have been out so late but neither of them cared and no one told them what to do. They'd spent the last 2 months avoiding school, avoiding their parents and basically doing whatever they wanted.

Not so long after finishing the last cans of lager, the boy's restlessness was tripping over into devilment. This was a familiar pattern that the residents of Dowderthwaite were thoroughly sick of. Behind the spot where they were holed up was Dowderthwaite bowling club and many of the members of the club had suffered Keiron and Dan's misbehaviour. As far as the boys were concerned, they were being picked on and had been since they were little children.

"Don't climb the fence!"

"Don't run through my garden!"

"Stop pulling up the flowers!"

And there was a constant stream of protestors at their parents' doors complaining about the boys' behaviour. Mrs Metcalfe was always apologetic, Mrs Carter made no apologies. "Boys will be boys," she would say and go back to reading her magazines.

Thus, faced with years of scrutiny, disapproval and tacit approval from their parents, Dan made a suggestion that got Keiron chuckling.

"I reckon," said Dan, slurring a little, "that those interfering old gits could do with a lesson."

"What d' yer mean?" replied Keiron a little lost in a haze of Stella Artois.

"Yer know, Mr and Mrs Grosman for one. Constantly on our case. I can't fart without her scowling at me and that's from 1,000 yards away."

Keiron was chuckling. "Aye, but what lesson then?"

"You see that club house, over yonder," he suggested. "Reckon we should break in and steal their bowling balls and chuck 'em in the river."

"You're mad. Off yer rocker," said Keiron smiling.

"I am, I'm mental and I'm sick of 'em." And suddenly, he jumped to his feet. "Come on!"

"Sssshh!" said Keiron. "You'll wake the whole village!"

Quickly he got to his feet and followed his friend. They both stole quietly to the rear of the clubhouse. It was a timber building built around the end of Queen Victoria's reign. It had a pretty veranda with a double-fronted face. When Dan tried the door, it wasn't going to give in easily but with his gutting knife, he managed to prise open the lock and they were in. Once their eyes had adjusted to the dark interior, they found rows and rows of square pigeon holes all filled with bowling bags with the names of their owners stamped on the front. It was not hard to spot Mr and Mrs Grosman's equipment. Dan grabbed the bag and having put the knife back into his pocket, brought something else out.

"I've got a better idea," said Dan. "Let's burn 'em instead." And without warning, grabbed the bag and tried to light it with his cigarette lighter.

"Not in 'ere!" wailed Keiron but it was already too late. The old leather bag, with its cotton and card interior, was already alight and soon too hot for Dan to hold. He dropped it onto the carpeted floor.

"Fuck!" he said. "'s' hot!"

"Bollocks! It's catching on the carpet!" shouted Keiron. They started to stamp on the flames but they both knew they were making a racket and their efforts were in vain.

"Let's get out of 'ere!"

Without a thought, they bolted through the door and ran off, disappearing into the surrounding countryside leaving all their equipment and detritus on the river bank.

They were gone for 3 days and by the time they had snuck back home, the bowling club house was a pile of ash and it didn't take the detective powers of Sherlock Holmes to work out who was to blame.

Within 24 hours, they were arrested and in due course, charged and convicted of malicious damage and then put firmly in the hands of the youth justice system.

Dan blamed Keiron for the whole episode and Keiron being drunk, couldn't fully recall what had happened and therefore, had no legitimate evidence or reason to deny it. Mrs Carter then took the opportunity to point the finger at Keiron and when the opportunity arose, no matter how slight, she would remind anyone who would listen who was to blame. Soon the villagers were picking up their pitchforks and demanding Keiron's head on a stake.

Keiron then took charge of things for himself. He was a competent 'Bush-man', he loved wild camping, poaching and lighting fires so he disappeared again into the North Yorkshire countryside. Not for 3 days this time but for 2 weeks.

When he returned home after his second jaunt away, his mum was frantic with worry. His disappearance had made the papers, and even the neighbours had been scouring the local woods. The police had patrolled the countryside and dredged the bottom of the Dowderdale River. Keiron's reappearance was arousing both joy and anger.

Faced with the mood in the village, social services stepped in to get Keiron out of Dowderthwaite and give him and his family some respite. He was sent into foster care on the East Yorkshire coast and spent the remaining summer months keeping his head down, playing on the amusements and eating ice cream.

After 6 weeks away, the day he slipped back home and into his bedroom, no one noticed but it was now up to social services and the school to decide the best options for Keiron as he would be expected back in education at the beginning of September. This is where I come into his story because the decision they made was to use work experience as the main route to student engagement.

Ms Salbanio, deputy head of his school had called me in to review Keiron's case. She was in her mid-40s, well dressed, slim with a bob of brown hair. She had a kindly face but it was obvious, she regularly contorted it into a snarl to make a student stop and pay her immediate attention. She explained Kieron's situation, painting a dour picture of misbehaviour and describing what I could only imagine was an out-and-out ruffian. I was nervous about meeting Keiron and when she told me he did boxing as a hobby, I quickly changed my opinion of him, he wasn't a ruffian; he was an out-and-out hooligan.

My first encounter with him couldn't have been any different from my imagination. He was polite, intelligent and welcoming. However, as with common teenage protocol, he was still in his pyjamas at 1 pm in the afternoon watching TV and when I surveyed him carefully, I could see deep cuts and scratches on his hands and arms. I imagined him stooping through brambles and thorns to get to his den while he was on the run. He also had the odd homemade tattoo on his hands; just little lines where he'd started and given up, either due to the pain or a lack of artistic ability. He was also a typical spotty youth, with red patches on his face and pimples everywhere. To complete the hooligan ensemble, he had his hair cut short like an old-time prisoner of war, emphasising a rawness to his character that was at odds with his polite and friendly manner. He also had the biggest watch I'd ever seen, sat squarely on his left wrist like a box of cornflakes. It was so incongruous in this setting and on this lad.

"Nice watch," I lied.

"Cheers," he replied. "Got it for me 15th birthday. Goes down to 50m."

"Useful," I said. His eyes were glued to the TV above the fireplace. It had a 50" screen and was far too big for the room. I looked around and found it to be busy with ornaments, phone cables, clothing and shoes and there in the corner, a can of Febreze. I couldn't smell it but I gagged involuntarily regardless.

"Right, Keiron," I said, "do you know why I'm here?"

"Aye, work experience," he replied.

"Do you mind turning the TV off please?" I asked.

"Oh sorry yeah," he said and promptly pressed the remote control. "Extreme downhill cycling. One day I'm going to enter the 'Ard Rock Enduro," he declared.

Of course you are, I thought. The 'Ard Rock Enduro was an up-and-coming event that was to become one of the UK's premier off-road cycling courses, full of swooping down hill sections, skittish skips through boulders and trees with a final heart-pounding flourish to the finish.

"Have you thought about what type of work experience you might want to do?" I asked, wanting to move the conversation on. Dowderthwaite was miles away from anywhere and I had other people to see.

He spun around to face me as his watch wobbled precariously on his arm.

"Owt outside would be good," he said with enthusiasm. And it was genuine, whatever had brought him to this point he'd overcome it and it was clear he was looking forward to work experience with gusto.

"I want to be a tree surgeon one day, so something like that would be good." He checked his watch. It wasn't hard; its face was bigger than Big Ben.

"I don't mean to be rude but I'm due in the gym in half an hour," he said, cracking his knuckles and then arching his back in a cat-like stretch.

"I don't need a lot of time as it's clear you have a good idea what you want to do, so I'll leave you to it," I said and left the house as Keiron politely ushered me to the door.

I then drove the short distance to see Dan Carter. Dan was a different kettle of fish. He had managed to avoid the wrath of the villagers but the school wasn't so sure he was as innocent as Mrs Carter insisted. Therefore, they also put him in the work experience program. At no more than 5' 4" and skinny as a beanpole with a shifty look to his dark eyes, I concluded that Dan was going to be a more difficult customer.

His home was in the wealthier part of the village with neat borders and hedges and it was clear the Carters must have had good jobs to pay for it all.

Before I could enter the house, I was asked to remove my shoes by a very pristine Mrs Carter. Everywhere were cream carpets and rugs, so they were clearly very house proud. mum was a bright orange colour with manicured nails and expensively cut and dyed blond hair.

"How long will this take?" she asked. "I've got to go into town to pay the deposit for our holiday."

"About 20 minutes that's all," I replied, thinking to myself, why is everyone in such a rush when they meet me?

"Tenerife," she said. "We go at least 4 times a year," she added without any prompting.

"I could walk but I like to take the Mini. It's my little present to myself," she continued and glanced at my socks. Thank God I'd got a decent pair on. My mind wandered wondering whether Mrs Carter was walking to Tenerife or to town. I never found out.

"So what is the point of work experience for a lad like our Dan?" she asked. "I mean if it wasn't for that little scumbag friend of his, he would be in school full-time."

Her mask of respectability slipped just ever so slightly with her choice of words. She quickly composed herself for a reply but I resisted the temptation, as just then Dan walked in, eyes glued to his phone.

"This is Charlie, he's here to discuss work experience," she said with a hint of sarcasm and looked directly at me. "Good luck with that. As you can see, Dan's not the talkative type."

"OK, Dan, have you thought about what you might like to do?" I asked in hope.

The following 15 minutes were spent coaxing as much as I could from the master of the one-word answer. "Yes", "no" and "dunno" was all he could muster and all the while he was conducting a variety of tasks on his smartphone. Hopefully, it was some in-depth research for his homework but in reality, he was probably watching a host of irrelevant and pointless videos on YouTube.

His mum never intervened and as the clock spun around the full 20 minutes, she was getting restless. One of her tanned legs was already on the plane and the other was desperate to join it, so I left with little to go on other than the fact Dan wasn't the sharpest tool in the box but he may, therefore, be open to try anything, which could be a blessing.

Within a few days, Keiron's placement was organised, I'd sorted a job with a local landscape gardener and he would be expected to work 8 am to 4 pm, 2 days per week with 3 days in school. The placement started fantastically well, his employer was impressed by Keiron's enthusiasm and knowledge and was already getting him to measure up and take control of some of the more technically demanding jobs.

Dan's placement finding, however, was not going well. I would text him a suggestion and would receive abusive and foul-mouthed replies;

what point in that, you idiot
no way working in a fuckin shop

The boy clearly didn't have much of an imagination, even his insults were a struggle for him to master. Dan was clearly a telephone tough guy; as strong as 10 men over the phone and as weak as a newborn kitten in person.

Just as I was getting to grips with Dan's communication style, the rug was pulled from under my feet by Keiron. Ordinarily, Keiron was taken to work each day by taxi but that morning he had refused to get out of bed. His mum couldn't rouse him but she had to go to work, leaving Kieron alone to make his own choices. When I was told what had happened, I tried to ring him but he wouldn't answer his phone and neither would he come to the door when I went around a little later. I was just leaving the property when my phone buzzed. It was a text from Dan.

No bastard way work in garage

That was all I needed.

Over the next week, we had a hell of a time trying to pin down Keiron, he was at home but would slip out before his mum came home and slip back in when she went to bed. At the same time, I was also swatting off Dan's unimaginative but foul-mouthed text messages. I wasn't having much success with these 2 reprobates.

Eventually, however, Keiron's mum confronted him one morning by going into his bedroom and tipping him off his mattress. School's opinion of Mrs Metcalfe was that she was too soft but clearly the straw had broken the camel's back and she was now getting tough. To be fair, the lad had taken her to the edge of the reason so it was only a matter of time before she snapped.

"What the hell's going on, Keiron?" she yelled.

"Back off, mum," he replied. "Leave me alone!" He stood there in his pyjamas, bleary-eyed and dishevelled having been awoken so dramatically.

"Why are you not going to work?" she continued shouting.

"I don't like landscaping." His reply was weak and incomprehensible having specifically requested that type of job and mum wasn't putting up with that.

"Rubbish! Just tell me what's going on," she said.

Over the next half an hour, she managed to glean just enough to allow a conclusion to be drawn. It seemed that Keiron was struggling, with such a tight routine and long working hours, having spent the previous few months doing whatever he wanted. This tended to involve a lot of late mornings and even later nights. He was worn out, particularly as his boss delegated so readily to him. Not only was he physically tired but he was also mentally stressed with the thought of getting his measurements wrong. This was all very plausible and we had a duty of care to make sure the placement was both suitable and rewarding for Keiron. Therefore, I went to meet his boss and we agreed to reduce his hours to try and help him with the shock of working.

It didn't offer the intended outcome. Within 2 weeks, Keiron performed the same routine. He refused to get in the taxi and then went on a 3 day flit to avoid any confrontation.

In the meantime, however, I was making some progress with Dan. Having spoken to Mrs Carter again, she put me in touch with a family friend who offered to take Dan into his construction firm. Dan's whole demeanour changed; gone was the bravado and tough exterior, what remained was a young lad completely devoid of any communication skills or confidence whatsoever. No matter what the owner said, the only answer he could get from Dan was one syllable long. If the interview had been conducted via text, there may have been more opportunity for Dan to express himself but the idea of the boss receiving a text so devoid of thought and riddled throughout with expletives was enough to make me sweat.

It didn't matter though, as the employer had made Dan's mum a promise and offered him a placement anyway.

The coming weeks would see a marked difference in Dan's attitude. The team he was working with were very down-to-earth and they took to Dan immediately, mainly because he was the butt of all their jokes. Surprisingly, Dan coped very well with all the ribbing and with that, he earned their respect. This could be partly due to the fact that they were on a site 20 miles from home and he couldn't escape but I am more inclined to think that Dan had started to grow up a bit and not take himself too seriously. My visits tended to be humorous and enjoyable affairs and it didn't seem to matter what jobs Dan was doing so long as he was with his crew.

Today, Dan is still with that company, having gone on to take a full-time job. It seems to work that way in the building trade; ask your apprentice to fetch a long stand or a tin of tartan paint. If they can take the joke with grace, then they'll do alright. I can only conclude that Dan had found the role models he needed, after all his mum was so aloof and disinterested it seemed that Dan's behaviour was a cry for attention and he was now getting it in spades, literally.

For Keiron on the other hand, it was a make or break time. The taxi firm had refused to collect him anymore because they had to wait far too long for him to get out of bed. This had the inevitable knock-on effect on other jobs, which the taxi firm could ill afford to lose. This meant Keiron could no longer work with the landscape gardeners so I had to find a placement within walking/cycling distance of Keiron's home. The only chance of success I had was to find him a placement with someone who didn't know him and this was likely to be an impossible task considering his notoriety in the village. Added to this was the likelihood of Keiron refusing to do whatever it was that I could find for him.

However, by some improbable miracle, I managed it.

About 1 mile from Keiron's home was a large pig farm, housing as many as 3,000 pigs at any one time. Devoid of other options or ideas, I felt I had only this one chance to find Keiron a work placement. In order to give myself the best chance possible, I decided the best option would be to put on my wellies and visit the farm as early as I could as the morning is usually the best time as it is mucking out and feeding up time.

Although pigs have a reputation for being dirty, they are in fact very clean and tend to soil their pens in the same place.

Regardless of this fact, however, the pig smell is unbelievably overpowering. Throughout the site, the pigs were housed in small buildings set at approximately 20 degrees centigrade and almost 100% humidity. Entering one of these pens on a cold day in particular has an overpowering effect that no amount of Febreze could overcome. My glasses would mist up and I would feel dizzy with the rising ammonia. The first time I confronted John Calvert the owner of the farm, he was tending some new mothers in the farrowing pen. He seemed completely unfazed by the smell but was aware of my presence before I could open my mouth.

"Now then lad, what can I do for you?" he said, slowly standing up and turning around to face me. He was a tall balding man with hands the size of shovels and a face red with continued exposure to the elements, both meteorological and elemental.

I explained my reasons and when he replied, my optimism went stratospheric. I tried to remain calm.

"Aye, it sounds alreet t'me," he mused. "Who is this lad?"

I landed back on earth with a bump and took a deep breath. After telling him about Keiron, I envisaged being manhandled by those massive paws on the end of his arms, as he pushed me off his property.

"A young man called Keiron." I paused hoping he would accept just the first name. He leaned forward a bit more.

"Keiron who?" he said.

"Keiron Metcalfe," I replied.

"How old is 'e?"

"15."

"Where's 'e live?"

"Dowderthwaite."

"I know a load er Metcalfe's from up Dale but I've never heard of a lad called Keiron." He looked puzzled for a moment as if he was trying to calculate the square root of a 5 digit number. Something was nagging him.

"Nope, don't know him," he said with finality and my optimism rose again but to new heights. He didn't know him!

I decided that John was not a typical farmer, he wasn't interested in local politics or gossip and believe me that is almost nigh on incredible. A farmer not being interested in the local gossip! I'd won the lottery!

Pleased with my progress that morning, I jumped in the car with my wellies on and drove straight to Keiron's house. The smell of the farm was still overpowering even with the windows open and I didn't lose the aroma of pigs for at least a day.

However, when I met Keiron, the smell emanating from my wellies and the choice of placement didn't put him off, he was really pleased with the prospect of working with pigs and he proved it by turning up every day and staying well beyond his normal hours. Each time I visited him, he was growing in his knowledge of pig husbandry and John was really pleased with him.

On my last day working with Keiron, I went to the farm to meet him to say good luck. Keiron was very polite as normal. He was a pig in muck regarding his placement and rightly so as John had offered him a full-time job that would start as soon as he left school. He stood there with a big grin on his face and a fading bruise creasing the corner of his left eye. I guess the boxing wasn't going so well. I left him and wandered across the farm to find John and thank him for his patience.

"So, how have you got on with Keiron then, John?" I asked.

"Well, you know lad, he's been brilliant," he said. "I can leave 'im to his own devices. He just gets on wi' job, he dunt complain and no matter what the weather, 'e's allus 'ere on time."

"That's great to hear, John. You've made a massive difference to his life," I said in reply.

"I guess." He then stood a little to one side and looked across the farm into the fields.

"I reckon I've got t'point when I can trust 'im with most jobs," he continued and looked at me with a twinkle in his eye.

"But I don't think I'll be askin' 'im to polish me bowling balls any time soon."

Street Life

Ibrahim or Ibra for short, eased into the room like an uncoiling snake. He was 6' 4" tall, grew facial hair quicker than I could run to the shop, had dark eyes that bored into your soul and could command respect without saying a word. Not only that, he was a martial arts expert and tattooed from head to foot. Ibra was now my business partner and we had regular catch-up meetings to discuss student progress. Therefore, he had driven out to our offices to go through the cohort of students we supported. After easing around the door, he folded himself into a chair and huddled over his notepad.

The office was one of a large number of units in a converted Victorian factory. It was a serviced office which means that your post and phone calls are handled by a reception team working for a number of different businesses at any one time. This helps if you are out and about like Ibra and me, as we had the benefit of a back office to cover us when we couldn't answer queries. In theory any way.

In our wisdom, we had gone for the cheapest offices we could find. Therefore, they were poorly furnished and cold, with the IT system on the verge of collapse. An asthmatic chain smoker could generate more oomph than the broadband in our office. Secondly, the receptionist was totally disinterested in taking calls and when she did, they were often transcribed incorrectly so we had no idea who had rung. Weirdly, we quite liked the quirky environment and had stuck with it for the last 5 years.

Hunched over his notepad, Ibra began a monologue of depressing facts. "Toby, sacked. 2nd day. Abrar, sacked, wouldn't get out of bed. Lucy, sacked, took £5 from the till in the COOP for expenses. Before you ask, no police involvement. Just sacked off." And so it went on. We would go through our list of students highlighting the sackings, redeployments and new starters.

"I've got this really tough situation at the moment," he said, rolling back into his chair and placing his hands behind his head. His arms were long and slim with a full sleeve tattoo on each side. He looked like an Arabian pirate. He then stared at me with his dark, almost menacing eyes.

"The thing is, it's this lad, as soon as he turned 16, his mum and dad kicked him out. They said they would but he didn't believe them." Fortunately his mouth didn't match his eyes; it was kind and ready to laugh at the slightest provocation. He chuckled a bit.

"Can't see what's so funny, Ibra," I said.

"Nothing is," he replied. "It just got me thinking that he's on the streets but is still desperate to keep his placement. He's spent the last 2 nights in a recycling bin at the back of the supermarket but he still turns up for work on time."

"Where's he working?" I asked.

"Dindo's Chicken Shack, so at least he gets a couple of meals. Funny really what motivates people. You'd think he'd be depressed but he hasn't got time for that. He's so desperate to find a roof over his head."

"What can the school do?"

"Not much. We think we've found a hostel for him but the problem is he has nothing of value as he left home with nothing." He paused and pondered the situation for a minute then continued. "Can we pay for a few bits of clothes and toiletries to help him out?" he asked.

I didn't pause for thought. "Sure, we can't have that on our conscience."

We operated *The Work Project* on a not-for-profit basis, so if we felt the situation justified it, we would clothe, feed and give money to students to help them. Ironically, we'd applied for grants and funding but all to no avail; we weren't profitable enough to invest in.

Ibra definitely had the tougher job. His students were the more desperate, more neglected and traumatised group than mine. They lived in the big inner city, with proper gangsters and drug dealers, not the great pretenders I had to deal with. One young lad Ibra supported held down a job in a timber yard during the day and delivered drugs at night. He drove a white transit van with blocks on the pedals so he could work them properly. Ibra would simply ensure the work placement was a success and keep well clear of the clandestine activities.

However, Ibra's experience with the homeless student is not unique to him. One of my students Zephr had endured a really tough time. Fortunately, she didn't end up on the street but the outcome of the sorry affair was due in the main to her overbearing and demanding grandmother.

Zephr Mcpherson was the oldest of three children and when her mum and dad split, the whole family ended up at opposite ends of the country. Dad moved down south with work and mum moved back to Scotland to be with her family.

Zephr being in her teens wanted to stay in Yorkshire and went to live with her grandmother who I first met when Mrs Salbanio asked me to find Zephr a work placement in a childrens nursery. Mrs Salbanio had warned me that Maureen was an abrasive character and it became abundantly clear that she felt Zephr had been neglected by the school.

When I arrived at the house and rang the doorbell, I was met with a cacophony of sounds from at least 3 barking dogs. They appeared briefly in the window as they bounced up and down on the spot. Eventually, a number of locks were undone and the door opened slowly to stop any of the dogs from escaping. What did escape, though, was a cloud of smoke as thick as December fog. I was ushered inside by Maureen with 3 dogs snapping at my heels.

"Don't mind dogs, do yer?" she snapped. *Yes, I do,* I thought.

"No, they're fine," I said as the dogs continued to bounce around in a haze of cigarette smoke. Clearly, Maureen wasn't going to put the dogs out of the way and wasn't going to stop smoking either. The smell of dogs and cigarette smoke was overpowering and there in the background miasma, trying to mask the smell, was a hint of Febreze. At least the TV was switched off I thought and gagged a little.

"Zephr! Zephr!" She bellowed. "That bloke from school's 'ere 'bout work experience!"

"She'll be darn in a minute," she added. "Struggles to get out er bed before 10."

Interesting, I thought, as it was 12:30 pm. Why is she still in bed and not at school? Eventually, the living room door opened and in she walked. It was more of a shuffle than a walk. Head down, clothes unkempt, holes in her socks.

"Here she is," tutted Maureen. "I don't know why we bother. She should be in school doing her exams, not at home in bed." It was said for my benefit I thought, rather than Maureen really giving a damn.

"She's a bright girl," she continued, "but no! Mrs Salbanio dun't think Zephr can do her exams, does she? So what are you going to do for her?" She didn't pause for breath. "I'll tell you what you'll do. If she has to do work experience, she does summat meaningful, wi' prospects."

"Mrs Salbanio suggested working in a nursery," I replied. "She's already spoken to Zephr about what she wants to do."

"Is that so?" She turned to face Zephy and drew heavily on her cigarette. "What are you gunna learn workin' there? For God's sake, can't you do summat wi' more goin' for it?"

"Like what?" squeaked Zephr.

"Like…well I don't know. What do you suggest?" She turned to me again.

"Whatever Zephr is interested in," I said hesitantly. "Work experience is as much about developing a good routine as well as work skills."

"Rubbish! She needs to learn summat useful. Ideally like her GCSEs!" she exclaimed. Fag ash fell after teetering on the edge of her cigarette. She just casually rubbed it into the carpet while the dogs looked on.

Faced with such strong opinions, I wasn't going to make much more progress. So I left making promises I couldn't guarantee just to get out of there, namely a placement with prospects. However, I did arrange to go see Mrs Salbanio in school, followed by a brief meeting with Zephr to get to know her a bit better.

The meeting with Mrs Salbanio was short. In the school's opinion, Zephr was too fragile to maintain regular and meaningful attendance in school and therefore, needed a very supportive placement. Her relationship with her mother had been tempestuous particularly as her mum was an alcoholic. Watching her mum descend rapidly into a stupor had left Zephr feeling very vulnerable. Her grandmother then exacerbated the problem as she blamed Zephr's mum for the breakup of the family. Maureen naturally sided with her son, Zephr's dad – he could do no wrong.

My meeting with Zephr confirmed the school's prognosis that she was very vulnerable; she had no interest in school and felt intimidated by the atmosphere. Her attendance that day was because Maureen had driven her and without that push, she would still be at home in bed.

"So how are you?" I asked knowing our conversation was likely to be difficult.

"Fine," she replied, almost imperceptibly.

"Miss tells me that you would like to do work experience in a nursery. Can you explain why?" I continued.

"Well," she hesitated, "when a lived wi' me mum, I used to have t'look after Luke and Daniel, me twin brothers. I enjoyed it but now they're in care because me mum couldn't look after 'em properly."

"Why are they not living with you now?" I asked, almost knowing the answer.

"They're in foster care," she said.

"They went into care when me mum went back t'Scotland t'live with me other Nan but Nan Mcpherson can't cope wi' 'em, even though I've offered t'help as much as a can. She says I need to be in school rather than be looking after two babies."

"How old are they?" The question was almost pointless, I couldn't help the situation but I was hoping I could keep the conversation going a bit longer.

Tears started to well up in her eyes; her dilated pupils unseeing, almost searching.

"They'll be 18 months old now," she said.

"OK, I'm sure you'll see them every now and again."

"Yes," she said, wiping her face, and sniffing. "Every so often."

"Right, well look," I said as breezily as I could. "Let's try and get you a placement as soon as we can and as part of that, we'll document all the things you do so we can put together a CV and then maybe get you a job?"

She nodded in agreement.

"I'll speak to a few pre-school nurseries and get you something suitable." And with that, we ended our discussion.

I was now left with a bit of a dilemma. I had a vulnerable young girl who couldn't cope with life on the one hand and on the other, I had an overbearing Nan with lofty expectations.

Now one thing we have in our armoury is the opportunity to offer students a package of employability qualifications. Although not recognised alongside GCSEs, they are useful for colleges and employers as they recognise the skills learnt as part of the work experience package.

But before I could even propose this option, and barely 2 hours after I met with Zephr, Maureen was on the phone.

"You've met with her again then," she barked. "So where's she gunna be workin'?" Her frustration was clearly bubbling to the surface.

"I don't know yet," I replied. "I need to make sure she's going to be comfortable with the people she will be working with."

"Well that's not good enough, she needs t'know where she's workin' as soon as possible and I need t'know so I can sort out me own day out," she snapped.

"I'm sorry," I offered. "But it doesn't happen that quickly. There's a lot to consider."

"Well, I can't see what all this fuss is about," she said. "At the end of the day, Zephr should be in school doin' her exams, not messin' wi' babies in a nursery. What exactly is she gonna learn there?"

This was my chance I thought. "There is one thing, Mrs McPherson. I'll go through an employability qualification with her to document all that she learns as she is doing her placement."

"Employability qualification!" she quipped. "Not the same as proper exams and not the same as an apprenticeship!"

"I'm sorry you feel like that but other students have found it useful," I said in hope more than confidence.

"Other students?" she shouted. "Are they thick or summat? My granddaughter is not doin' any qualification suited for thickos. I saw all that employability stuff when I taught nurses before I retired."

I was wilting under the force of her opinion but with some effort, I tried to counter.

"Hold on a minute, Mrs McPherson, these students aren't stupid, they're just not ready for GCSEs or they just don't get on with school."

She ignored me completely. "My Zephr is not doin' that. End of…" And promptly slammed down the phone. I could imagine a volcano slowly easing back into hibernation having erupted violently into the air. In this case, clouds of smoke billowing from Maureen McPherson's mouth, reduced to tendrils and whisps.

In the next week or so, I put my efforts into finding Zephr a placement and was lucky to find the perfect match, a nursery not too far from her home with an extensive service for babies only months old right through until school age. The building was a 4 storey Victorian home, converted into separate facilities based on the age of the children. On the ground floor were the young babies, going up to the top floor for children aged around 4 years old.

I introduced Zephr to the owner Kelly who, in her wisdom, decided to put Zephr with the young babies under her personal supervision. The first few weeks went very well. Nan took Zephr each day and Zephr spent her time in the comforting atmosphere of the early years' facility. My visits were fairly brief and conversations with Zephr basic and perfunctory.

Because I felt I wasn't really connecting with Zephr, I had a conversation with Kelly who felt that there may be a benefit in moving Zephr onto the next level, literally. This would mean working with older children. However, we agreed that this should take place a bit further down the line when Zephr had had more opportunities to meet other staff and become comfortable with them.

I was happy with the decision but this was completely steam-rollered by Mrs McPherson.

"I've been ter't nursery," she hollered down the phone. "I've had a word wi' manager."

"You did what?" I said with surprise; surprised at my own indignation. I could imagine the volcano was going to spew forth again.

"I told her I would like to see Zephr get an apprenticeship out of this placement. No point going if she dun't." she barked.

"I'm sorry, Mrs McPherson," I countered, "but it's too early to ask for that commitment. Also, Zephr is only just starting to engage with the other staff. I would think this is going to take more time than you would like."

"Look, young man," she responded, patronisingly, "I believe you don't get owt in life wi' out askin'. Zephr's a bright girl; she just needs a little push. No 'arm in findin' out what 'er prospects are."

A push, more like a shove off a cliff! That's what I wanted to say but replied as diplomatically as I could. "Well I'm afraid I don't think it's wise to try too hard now, I would advise we work a little slower with Zephr."

"We'll see," she said with finality. "And another thing. I don't want you fillin' 'er 'ead wi' any of that employability stuff, she needs to be thinkin' about doin' her proper exams." The phone went dead and all I could do was feel sorry for poor Zephr having to live with a constantly burping volcano.

The next time I saw Kelly, she was pretty unhappy that Mrs McPherson had been so direct. I tried to explain that she was always like that and I would try and placate her if I could. She did however hint that they do take apprentices and that Zephr may be considered if she does some form of qualification as they would normally expect prospective employees to have at least maths and English GCSEs. I pointed out that there was an alternative and would she consider it? Kelly gave it some thought over the next few days and let me know via email that she would be happy for Zephr to go through the employability program but how was I going to explain that to Mrs McPherson?

I decided to contact Ms Salbanio at school and explain my dilemma. She was obviously sympathetic and said she would speak to Mrs McPherson herself as she is less abrasive with her. After a day or so, Ms Salbanio rang to say that she had spoken to Zephr's Nan and she had explained the opportunities for Zephr, however, Mrs McPherson insisted that instead of working on my programme, she was demanding that Zephr attend school to do Maths and English. With regret, Ms Salbanio had agreed to help Zephr try and get her Maths and English grades.

In some respects, this shouldn't really affect me as school was going to play an active role in getting Zephr the appropriate qualifications. But things were never going to run that smoothly.

On my next visit to see Zephr, it was just after half term and she had therefore had a week off. I took her for a coffee at the local supermarket so we could have a chat because by now, she had begun to trust me. I asked her how she was and opened up quite readily.

"Fine, I've just been to see me mum in Scotland," she said.

"Oh, I hope that went OK," I replied.

"Not so great," she said. "Unfortunately, she's drinking a lot and is in tears all the time about the twins. I couldn't get away quick enough."

"That sounds awful," I responded with sympathy.

I knew what it was like to be in a similar situation.

"How are you enjoying work?" I asked.

"It's OK, I like the babies as they remind me of the twins," she said and started to drift off into her own thoughts.

"How would you like to move on and work with toddlers instead? It will help with your experience." I asked.

She was now looking into the middle distance when she answered. "I'm not sure, it depends."

"Depends?" I asked. "On what?"

She took no notice of my question and changed the subject.

"I can't go into school. I just don't wanna. I know I'm gunna fail. What's the point?" Tears began to well in her eyes.

"You might not if you try," I offered.

She was crying now and was attracting the attention of other diners around us. I didn't say anything for quite a while until she gained her composure.

"Nan is on me case to get up and go to school. If she dun't leave me alone, I'm not goin' anywhere," she said eventually.

"Maybe if I tell school this, she might leave you alone. Would you want that?" I asked.

"I suppose so," she replied and carried on looking out of the window.

"If you do that, then in order to get a chance of an apprenticeship, will you be willing to do the employability program?" I said.

"I think so. Don't think Nan would be 'appy though," she said with resignation.

"Look, Zephr," I said with as much reassurance as I could, "this is about your opportunities and what's right for you now. For example, you could take your GCSEs as part of your apprenticeship or do them at college. Right now, you need to get your life as settled as you can and try and remain positive, particularly as work is quite settled."

She nodded in agreement and when I let the school know about our discussion, they weren't surprised and would let Nan know. Within minutes, my phone was ringing.

"What have you been puttin' in Zephr's head?" She growled like one of her dogs.

By now, I was used to her style and was becoming accustomed to the fact that nothing would placate the woman. Faced with that realisation, I was becoming more inclined to just tell her as it is.

"The fact is, Mrs McPherson, Zephr is extremely vulnerable. She is struggling to cope with the absence of her mum and her illness and is really struggling with the twins being in foster care. The last thing she needs is to be pushed, she needs encouragement. My plan, therefore, is to encourage her to take her own steps forward."

It was very quiet on the other end of the line. I faintly heard her draw on her cigarette, filling the room with smoke. I felt sorry for the poor dogs living in that environment.

"Reight," she said finally, "what does that mean?"

"Well," I paused briefly to gather my thoughts. This was an unusual situation; I was actually leading the conversation.

"We let Zephr tell us when she's ready to progress."

"Well she won't," she countered quickly. "She's too soft. I know 'er better than you."

I couldn't argue with her assessment but I was sure I knew what Zephr needed right now.

"At the end of the day, Mrs McPherson, all I can do is talk to her. She's not going to go into school, so we may as well accept that and try and work with her in the nursery."

"She's not goin' to get anywhere in life hidin' away," she said. "She needs to realise she needs to earn a livin' and get a career."

"I appreciate that but I don't want to push her and if I do, I have to be careful. Surely you can appreciate that?" I was trying to reconcile with her but she did not see the value in meeting me half way. She'd made her mind up.

"I'll make sure she goes to the nursery and get 'er apprenticeship," she said. I didn't know what that meant; she obviously had her own agenda. "I'll drop her off myself tomorrow." And with that, the discussion ended.

Knowing Zephr was in the next day I went to see her. We were given a small room on the top floor of the nursery to have our discussion.

"Are you ready to discuss some of the employability skills modules?" I asked.

"No. I'm not," she said. "Nan din't want me to do it before and now she's insistin' on it. I'm confused by it all."

"What about moving on with the other children?" I continued. "Working with the toddlers?"

"I don't want to," she said. "I just want t'stay wi' the babies."

With that, I knew that I had lost her. We had the opportunity to develop a future for Zephr but her Nan had interfered to the point where she had lost all motivation to work or learn.

The undoing of the program was fairly swift after that. Kelly made it clear that there was no chance of an apprenticeship unless Zephr got more involved. Based on that pressure, Zephr stopped attending. Before long, school withdrew support for the programme altogether and Zephr was left with nothing. Within days, she had fallen out with her Nan and was sofa surfing at her friends' houses and with that, had drawn the attention of social services. It was only because her mum had finally started to rehabilitate that Zephr was able to move on by going to Scotland. I sincerely hope the family is finally reunited one day.

As for Mrs McPherson, now she no longer has her granddaughter to worry about, I hope she's able to settle into her retirement in peace. However, I would expect that instead, she will find someone else to fall out with and God forbid anyone who does cross her path. It's not often you get the chance to experience a volcano exploding from such close range and survive.

Tell Me Sweet Little Lies

Dominic was described as a very bright, very mature young man by his mum but manipulative by school, who had referred him to me around Easter time. I then met him over the holiday and discovered he was a tall, thin lad with a pinched face, round eyes and a mouth full of braces. He was an orthodontist's dream. After a less than constructive meeting where he expressed little enthusiasm for anything, I offered him a placement in a shop. However, he was very non-committal. It seems his only long-term plan was to stay alive and get his teeth straightened. Although he showed as much enthusiasm as a pall bearer carrying a coffin, he did actually turn up to his placement which was a surprise but his ability to surprise me even further didn't take long to surface.

It was one of those days where both Ibra and I were doing paperwork in the office when Ibra took a call on the landline. He looked up from his computer and lifted the receiver. All I could hear was Ibra grunt a few times before passing me the phone.

"It's for you," he said. "I didn't quite get their name but they're not happy." He fixed me with one of his stares, raised his eyebrows and then resumed his work.

I reached for the handset slowly and it didn't take long for me to work out who it was.

"It's chuffing boring!" said the voice. It was Dominic Tordoff. "Boring!" he exclaimed again and this time, I caught the slight lisp due to the braces fitted to his teeth. "I'm learning nowt. What am I going to end up as, doing this sort of rubbish?"

"It's about learning a good routine," I replied. "Such as getting out of bed on time, going to work on time, doing as you're asked." Then with a startling realisation, I had a premonition things were even worse than simply Dominic being bored. Even Ibra sensed the tension as he listened in on the conversation.

"What phone did you call me on?" I said.

"The one in the manager's office, why?" he asked quizzically.

"Dominic. Where's Jez the manager?" I asked.

"He's right behind me. He wants to speak to you when I'm finished."

Oh, God. I bet he does.

"Right, Dominic. Can you put him on and go back to work?" I was sinking lower into my chair.

"I'll put him on," he replied, "but I'm not going back to work, it's boring, I'm off home."

The phone went silent and I could hear Dominic muttering something to Jez and then leave the room. Jez must have closed the door then and I could hear him slowly pick up the phone.

"Did you hear all that?" I whispered urgently to Ibra. He nodded in my direction and at the same time, Jez took a breath to speak. I didn't give him a chance. "I'm mortified, I've never had a student be so blatantly rude," I said.

"It's alright," he replied. "Obviously, Dominic needs more stimulation than stocking shelves but if you could vet the students a bit better next time, I would appreciate it. The staff here don't appreciate being looked down upon by a stroppy 15-year-old."

My face was now red with shame, and Ibra was trying his hardest not to burst out laughing at my discomfort. I tried not to look at him.

"Sorry, Jez, I really am. Dominic gave me the impression he would try anything," I lied but continued, "and I thought some experience in retail would do him some good. I really am sorry."

"No problem," he said, letting me off the hook and he put down the phone.

I put down the receiver and counted to 5 by which time Ibra was laughing heartily.

"I can't believe he did that in front of his boss!" he said between big gulps of air. His eyebrows almost jumped off his face. "Got yourself a livewire there, haven't you?"

"Thanks, pal," I replied.

"No bother, anytime!" he said.

Having been faced with such brutal honesty, I knew I would have to play it safe with Dominic in the future. My preference would have been to drop him like a hot brick but school was desperate for me to work with him. Dominic had an incredible level of intelligence but used it in a manipulative, rather than constructive fashion. He had given up on school because he'd decided there was no point, so as much as he could argue about politics and philosophise about life, he could hardly write his name. He was also economical with the truth, not so much a liar, he just avoided telling you the whole tale and yet, when he wasn't happy you got a whole barrelful of honest feedback.

Faced with having to continue working with him, I arranged a meeting with his mum Nikita, to try and get some idea of Dominic's interests. She was working in a Healthcare Shop in Penborough town centre and we met on a warm day in the market square. Dominic's mum was very well-spoken and sat opposite me on a pleasantly sited park bench. Nikita spoke very highly of Dominic; she described the lack of engagement she had from school, the lack of understanding regarding his needs and the lack of appreciation for his anxiety and borderline depression. She chose her words very carefully, and as with anyone who is well-spoken, you almost become subservient to their point of view.

School had described Dominic the way I encountered him, manipulative and judgemental so I was facing conflicting emotions from the conversation. She was so convincing that I came down firmly on the side of helping Dominic achieve his massive potential. Nikita swore she had great faith in my ability to help him and made a suggestion that he would work very well with a building friend of hers. He was working on a house refit about a quarter of a mile down the road, so after our meeting I rang him and went to the site.

The upgrade was on a Georgian house that at some time in the past had been a shop and was being refitted back to its original use but with a modern flavour. There was a lot going on with various tradesmen and labourers scurrying around fitting, building, plastering and measuring. The foreman was more than happy with the extra pair of hands and we agreed to start Dominic as soon as possible.

He'd been there about a month when I drove over to Penborough on a warm spring day. I parked in the small lane behind the property and stepping over planks of wood, scaffolding and discarded cans of soda I called through the back door.

Nigel Steadman or Nas to his friends welcomed me with a bit of a scowl. "He's not turned in this morning," he said.

"You're joking," I replied. The warm happy feeling of the day evaporated away like mist on the inside of a car windscreen.

"If you want my opinion," said Nas, "he'll have buggered off to Spain with his mum and not told anyone."

I'd forgotten that Nas and Nikita knew each other but what was she doing in Spain I wondered? Nas was happy to fill me in.

"She goes regularly to Spain to run holistic yoga classes. All that mumbo jumbo to help well-healed clients reset their mojo," he said. "If you can find out if he's there at least we'll know he's safe."

"Absolutely," I replied. "School will go ballistic if he's gone on a jolly without telling them but at the moment this is a massive safeguarding problem if he's out of the country."

I thanked Nas and let him get back to work and immediately phoned the school and Nikita to find out what was going on. School was obviously anxious to find out where Dominic was but Nikita did not answer my calls. I had no choice but to send a text to her and hoped for the best. At about 5 in the afternoon, I got a reply.

> *"Dominic is poorly and staying with his dad on the other side of town. I sent an email to school to let them know."*

If that's the case, why would Nas say they were in Spain? The answer to questions like this can be answered quite easily by social media. It wouldn't take a genius to check out Nikita Tordoff and see if she had checked in to let all her friends know she was having a fantastic holiday.

Sure enough, she'd done just that and posted that she was checking in to Manchester Airport to fly out to Malaga. A day later, a nice picture of her and Dominic appeared slightly red-faced, a glass in hand, and smiling at the camera.

I do wonder to myself whether people are born stupid and stay that way, or whether they learn to be stupid as they grow older. Here was the evidence that she'd lied on her son's behalf and it became very clear that the manipulative side of her son was learnt from her. What I really didn't appreciate and still don't is that people like that don't care. They'll say whatever they need to, to justify their decisions and behaviours. I was left hoping that faced with this evidence, Dominic would be removed from the work experience program as I struggle working with people I distrust.

I was wrong; the school did threaten permanent exclusion but would continue with the program if Nas would have him back.

To my surprise, Nas did have him back and Dominic slipped back into work like nothing had happened.

Part of the reason that Nas had him back so readily was that he employed a stonemason called Benjy who had a suspiciously looking young apprentice who went by the name of Dillon. It was appropriate because Dillon had a knack for sleeping in and a penchant for smoking weed. Dillon's best friend was Dominic but unbeknown to me, they were 2 partners in crime.

What I learned much later was that Dillon was a year older than Dominic and was the major male influence over him. Benjy, his dad was by and large a loveable rogue, he earned money as quick as he could and spent it twice as fast. Dillon was becoming the spitting image of his father with a cheeky smile, an easy-going style who always had an eye for shortcuts through life. However, whenever Dillon was working with his dad, then he was staying out of trouble. Furthermore, Benjy was onsite more often, which suited Nas as Benjy was a skilled stonemason. Thus, if Dominic was onsite too then Nas was hoping that would keep Dillon happy, his dad happy and therefore everything would be good; an intricate web completely reliant on all the strands to have any stability.

The inevitable unravelling of that thread began when the job was coming to a close. Benjy had the opportunity to go over to Ireland to work on a building site being run by a relative and he was planning to go quite soon leaving his wife and children behind while he worked away.

Over the course of the next week, he would chat with me while I visited Dominic and on one of those days, he explained that he'd had a change of heart and would be taking Dillon with him. I never really gave it a second thought.

A week later I visited the site again and they were in the process of completing the garden landscaping, laying flower beds, a patio and planting trees. Nas was speaking to the owner when I arrived so I waited patiently until he'd finished his conversation. After saying hello, he got straight down to business.

"Dominic's not here," he said bluntly, "and his mum is definitely in the country so he's not in Spain while she does her yoga."

I was a bit perplexed so I rang Nikita and she answered straight away.

"Oh hi, Charlie," she replied, after I had explained why I was ringing. "Dom has been staying with Dillon and his dad over the past few weeks while they've been on that job, so I haven't really seen him that much. Let me try and find out what's going on."

"Why has he been staying with them?" I asked. "And did you know Benjy was due to go to Ireland soon to work on another job?"

"Oh," she said, "nothing to worry about, Dillon and Dom are the best of buddies and have been since they were at primary school. I'll ring Benjy and see if he can shed any light on the matter." She ignored my question about Ireland, said her thanks and rang off.

After letting the school know that Dominic had gone awol again, I waited for some answers which came in the form of a pretty lengthy text message from mum about an hour later.

"Dylan tells me that Dom went to stay with his dad when they went to Ireland but also that he had been suffering from a bad cold so hadn't been to work. He will be back at work next week."

At least it gave a reason for why Dom was absent but it was clear she didn't communicate with his dad and relied on others to keep track of Dominic. It was all a bit of an afterthought and I had some niggling doubts about the situation. I'd never met dad, he and mum were estranged, Dominic never talked about him and from what others had said, he was a waste of space. However, pinning down the manoeuvrings of the Tordoffs was like trying to catch butterflies with a hula hoop. Based on my misgivings, I told the school that I didn't believe a word of it and they invited me in for a meeting.

"Thanks for coming in at such short notice," said Ms Salbanio and she got straight down to business.

"So what do you know about the latest goings-on with the Tordoffs?"

I explained what I knew and waited patiently for a response. Ms Salbanio was the deputy head and wasn't going to suffer fools easily. It was a warm day and I felt like I was one of them with the sweat collecting under my arms and trickling down my back. The last time I had felt like this was 20 years ago, getting a roasting for bunking off a chemistry lesson.

"Right, well it seemed the sensible thing to do was to speak to Dominic's younger brother who's in Year 7," she said. "And do you know what he said?" she continued rhetorically not waiting for an answer. "That Dominic was in Ireland. The little shit is in Ireland with Dillon Riley. So do you know what I did then? I got Dillon Riley's younger sister into my office and do you know what she said?" I could clearly see what was coming but regardless, I still jumped when she spoke again. "That Dillon was in Ireland with his dad checking out a new building job for a few days and that Dominic was with them. What do you think of that?"

I was just opening my mouth to reply when she jumped in again. "Pissed off!" she blurted. "Like I am. All that work and patience and the little shit pisses off to Ireland and his mum, the lazy mare, covers up for him so she can have an easy life because while he's living somewhere else, she doesn't have to deal with him."

My nerves were jangling at the potty-mouthed monologue from Ms Salbanio who had stood up and was walking around the room with purpose. She returned to her seat and sat down slowly, calmly readjusting her demeanour as her face returned to its previous serene outlook. She wasn't having a go at me, she was on my side but I was in the deputy head's office. Enough to strike fear into the hardest of students.

"So what are we going to do?" She deliberately slowed the pace of her words and dropped the tone. She sounded sinister, another octave lower and she would have been bloody scary.

"It all depends," I said a bit hesitantly. "If you want him to stay on work experience and if Nas Steadman will have him back then there's a chance but that job is coming to an end. If Nas won't have him then I'm going to have to start again. Unfortunately, he picks and chooses what he wants to do and that isn't acceptable."

"Right," she said with finality. "I'm going to get them both in school and lay down the law. In the meantime, you see if this Nas bloke will have Dominic back."

With that, we broke up the meeting and I went to see Nas. Without hesitation, he said no and explained that with Benjy no longer working with him, there was no one to keep a tab on Dominic. Another employer bites the dust.

A week later, the Tordoffs had their meeting in school. During the meeting, Nikita insisted that she didn't know Dominic was in Ireland, she truthfully thought he was with his dad but as they didn't speak to each other, it couldn't be corroborated. Based on this intransigence, Ms Salbanio said she would think about the situation and let us all know her decision.

Within a day or so, I received an email from Ms Salbanio asking me to give Dominic one last chance. Work was the only thing he would engage with and therefore, I got on with the job of sourcing a suitable placement. Fortunately, it only took a couple of days to find a placement at a joinery workshop that manufactured window frames and door casings. I took Dominic along for his first day and from then on for about 2 weeks all went well until one morning, I had a text from mum to say that Dominic was ill and was having a bout of depression. The employer had a fantastic attitude to mental health problems as they had had other members of staff who had suffered similar issues. Therefore, they were very accommodating.

But as the days passed, I started to get twitchy about the placement and worried that he might lose it, so I asked his mum if I could see Dominic and possibly take him to work myself. She responded that it was probably a good idea because he was having some counselling for his problems and was improving. Therefore, if I was going to see him could I make sure he could leave work at 2 pm as he had an appointment.

What happened that day was strange, to say the least. I arrived at his home and knocked on the door only to find a complete stranger answer the door who had no idea who

Dominic was. I'd been to the address numerous times so I was almost questioning my sanity when I rang Dominic on his phone.

"I'm staying in town," he said, "while mum's in Spain."

"Who's at your house then? It is number 45, isn't it?" I asked.

"Oh, it's house sitters. mum's got some friends of hers to look after the place while she's away. If you come up to town and wait outside the Black Lion pub, I'll come out."

So mum was in Spain again while Dominic was supposed to be ill. I pondered this for a while and then drove the short distance to town where I waited a little while until he appeared around a corner in his work gear. He opened the door, crouched in the passenger seat and we set off.

"How are you then?" I asked.

"Oh fine," he replied.

"Your dad lives near the pub then?" I asked.

"No," he replied. "He lives in Belton." Puzzled, I continued the small talk.

"So whose house were you at last night then?" I asked.

"That's Dillon's; he's back from Ireland for a week so I've been with him. There's no way I was going to work while he was home. You don't even get paid and Dillon's making a fortune," he said.

My eyebrows must have leapt off my face, or at least they felt like they did. I tried to resume my composure.

"Are you ready for work today then?"

He turned to me with a puzzled expression and then smirked, flashing a broad metallic smile. His braces were clearly on show.

"Yeah," he continued. "But can I leave early this afternoon as I have an appointment?" he said.

"No problem," I replied. "Your mum said you had a meeting with the counsellor."

He didn't even hesitate when he said, "Counsellor? I don't know what you're on about."

By now, I was the one looking puzzled but he continued.

"I'm not going for counselling, I have an appointment with the orthodontist on York Parade. I'm having the braces on my teeth adjusted."

Take a Chance on Me

I entered the builder's merchant without really thinking about it. I had a number of places to visit that day but this was one of those companies with a well-known brand name that also offered full kitchen and bathroom suites as well as pipe fittings and electrical goods. I felt it was the type of place that would be really good for a student and it also offered me the chance to get a bit of advice about kitchen doors and worktops, as I was looking to change mine after they'd suffered ten years of hard labour being battered by my own children.

When I entered the building, I spoke to the first member of staff I encountered, who was refilling a shelf with stock. When I asked to speak with the manager, he asked me why and when I explained, he politely asked me to follow him to the counter.

"Dave," he called across to a man with receding hair who was talking with another staff member while eating a bacon sandwich.

Obviously not the most inconvenient time to call, I thought.

He looked across at us and replied, "Yeah, what is it?"

"This chap here wants to ask you about possible work experience," he answered.

Still looking straight at us, the manager responded.

"Tell him…" He paused like I wasn't there.

"…Tell him to make an appointment, I'm too busy." And with that, he continued munching on his sandwich and carried on talking with his colleague, who was by now finding something very amusing.

The shop worker just looked at me and raised his eyebrows with sympathy. I have rarely been so embarrassed in my professional career. The only other time I felt the same sense of embarrassment was the time when I spilt coffee all over my trousers and they were so wet I had to remove them and dry them on the radiator while I sat at my desk in my underpants. Fortunately, it was my office but when a colleague came in for a chat while I was sitting there trouserless, I was very conscious of my state of undress!

I left the building angry at being so humiliated by this idiot with a heightened sense of self-importance. He gave me no opportunity to explain the reason for my visit and neither did he offer me the courtesy to be spoken to directly. He must have assumed that I was the one looking for work experience and having made this judgement, decided he could puff out his chest and perform a bit of ritual humiliation.

The man had plenty of time. He worked in a shop where you are regularly interrupted by customers but he had made the classic mistake of being judgemental without actually gathering the facts first. I felt like a tramp who'd wandered into a Range Rover dealership having just won the lottery.

The incident reminded me of the 1980s when I witnessed first-hand the dismantling of my father's understanding of the world of work. He had been raised by his parents to learn a trade and marry someone who could bear him children. He trained to be a skilled boiler-maker and was a proud member of the boiler-makers union. However, he had trained for an industry that would disappear in a generation.

My dad was a militant member of the blue-collar power base that had been dismantled and crushed in the union wars of the 1980s. Even worse was the fact that militant working men without jobs were considered undesirables and were discriminated against by the establishment and then by other employers. They had lost everything, including my father who fell into depression, drinking himself to death bemoaning the loss of the world he grew up in.

Fast forward to today and discrimination is still there. It may be less blatant but ultimately, Dave the Builders Merchant had proven the point. It's easy to be dismissive and judgemental when you have the power.

In contrast to such off-hand dismissiveness, my experience as a teenager was quite different. It was not unusual to walk into an establishment and ask for work and more often than not, people would give you the time of day and be respectful enough to give you an answer. Now we have online application forms, emails, HR etc and therefore, a gilt-edged opportunity for those in positions of authority to ignore those in need.

Because of my experiences, I use more traditional ways to gain access to decision makers. Almost 100% of the time I will try to get a face-to-face meeting to discuss work opportunities and using this approach, I get the best results. Younger people don't seem to have learnt this skill, either due to their dependence on technology or because they are kept at arm's length by prospective employers. So, it is harder today for them to make the inroads that I can. Being able to help this way, using skills learnt when I was a teenager, is one of the main reasons I do the job I do.

Thankfully, there are some potential employers who are very receptive to the idea of helping a young student. The first time I met Archie Baldwin, it was obvious he was a man who cared. We talked about life, kids, school, and everything we had in common. Archie was a rough-haired, rough-faced man, with kind eyes and a thoughtful expression. He owned a small garage on the outskirts of town, specialising in body repairs and paintwork.

The student I had in mind for Archie was Kevin Macanally, a young man with a difficult past, having been removed from his mum when she was very young and he was still a baby. He was placed by social services with his grandparents, who he now called mum and dad. What made matters worse for Kevin was that his mum had married later, had 2 more children and settled down to family life without him. For this reason, Kevin was really suffering from attachment problems that were only starting to surface at the age of 15.

Archie could see Kevin was a bit troubled but he took him under his wing and was brilliant with him. He let Kevin do everything in the garage and taught him the kind of skills that went back generations to the original coach builders. Kevin finally had a father figure and someone he admired.

"It's all abart touch," Archie would say. "Run tha' fingers over it time and time again. Rub it and love it."

And Kevin followed that advice preparing the panels, sanding and spraying until the finish was as smooth as glass.

It amazed me how they managed to finish some of the jobs they did as I don't think Archie ever tidied up. Paper was everywhere stuck to pieces of masking tape, floating around on the breeze created by the air dryer in the spraying booth.

"Ah but," Archie would say, "it's them new-fangled phones. He's constantly on it. If he's goin' to get anywhere in life, he needs to put the bloody thing in his pocket when 'e's at work."

"I'm more bothered he might trip up over something in the garage, to be honest," I said looking around at the detritus. It was a tinderbox. "I'll have a word with him."

Kevin never took any notice though. It was a constant battle between them but the arguments were more light-hearted than serious. Archie was somehow stuck in the past and didn't see the point of a lot of the modern technology we take for granted and Kevin was hooked on it.

It was about 6 weeks later when my phone rang around 9 pm in the evening. I wouldn't normally answer at that time but I could see it was Archie's number so I answered the phone to find him sounding rather agitated.

"'Ello, is that Charlie?" he said. "I've got summat to tell yer."

"What is it?" I asked.

"I can't 'ave 'im no more," he continued. "I've got things goin' on that I can't cope with."

"What do you mean?" I replied.

"It's not 'im, it's me. I just can't have 'im."

My mind was racing somewhat. I didn't really want to get into an in-depth conversation at that time of night.

"OK, maybe I could pop around tomorrow morning and we can have a chat about it," I offered.

"Aye lad, come round in the mornin' and we can talk," he said.

I went down to the garage at about 10 am. Archie was in his office, his face pale, his expression distant and his hair as ruffled and unkempt as ever. The office was extremely disorganised, in fact, there was no order whatsoever to the bills or the orders. There were tins of paint, old calendars from over 10 years ago, he had no computer, no chair, a lot of the mail was unopened and there were bits of paper and masking tape strewn across the floor. It said a lot about the man's state of mind but the reality of it became a bit of a shock.

"I took this business over from 'owb Bob who'd had it for years," he said in a soft voice, his hands running through his hair. "Taught me everything I know about cars and boats. Owt that needed body work he knew about it and taught me the skills."

"So why can't you have Kevin anymore, you know he looks up to you so much and has the talent?" I said.

"That's exactly it," he said. "I'm a failure, I've got a gas bill the size of a telephone number and I can't pay it. A useless wife, a run-away daughter and me car's knackered. The fact is"—he paused and screwed up his face a little—"I've got depression and the lad doesn't deserve to be around me when I'm like this."

The words hung in the air like a fog.

"Don't worry, I'm on medication," he continued. "But when I've got it bad, I can't see the point in anything." He looked at me then, a slight hint of fear in his eyes.

His honesty was so disarming, only then did I really appreciate the sacrifices he had made to help Kevin out.

"The missus, she's no bloody good," he continued angrily. "Sat on her fat arse all day while I slog me guts out 'ere. Me daughter spending half her life bunking off school and then me car. I pranged it pretty bad and it set on fire on the high street going shopping."

My God, I thought. He's had a run of bad luck.

"The black dog is summat I'll always have and I just need some time off. I'm getting counselling sessions startin' next week. Should be off work for about a month."

I was pretty shocked and didn't really know what to say. I'm not a counsellor and I'd never heard that expression before. Black Dog. It hung over Archie like a fog and then it struck me that the Black Dog had also hung over my father. It made me think of my dad in a different light. What if he had confronted his problems like Archie did? How different would things have been?

"How big's your gas bill?" I said sounding ridiculous but it seemed to snap Archie back to life.

"Bloody massive!" he exclaimed. "Goes back 5 years. They've estimated it and it's over 8 grand! I've already disputed it but I'm on the phone for hours arguing with 'em. No one can give me a straight answer and no one seems to care. The thing is, it's not my fault, the bloke in the unit next door changed his supplier and that's when I stopped getting bills. I've had to get a solicitor involved. He reckons I can negotiate a figure and a payment plan, so I don't need to worry. He can say what he likes but it's driving me mad."

"God!" I replied. My communication was somewhat limited by my shock. "At least it sounds like you're getting it sorted."

"Aye," he said, "but look at me motor."

Only then did I notice the Lancia Delta Integrale pushed up to the back of the workshop half-covered in paper, with dust already starting to settle on the panels. I still couldn't understand how Archie had managed to perform such miracles with bodywork in such a tip.

"She looks a bit sad," I said.

"Aye lad," he said and walked into the workshop, with me following behind. "I can fix the panels but there was an injector leak I reckon, that caused a fire under the bonnet. It's gonna take a bit of fettlin'."

"Can you do it?" I asked.

"Oh aye, no problem," he said with a hint of optimism. And then with some surprise, he asked, "What's gonna 'appen to Kev?"

"I'll have to tell him the placement has ended but I won't tell him the truth. You don't need that. I'll tell him you don't have the insurance or something like that. Then I'll have to find him something else," I said.

"OK," he grunted. "He was a good lad. Hopefully, you can find him summat similar."

Sadly, I didn't. I put him in motor retail and he hated it. He would constantly ask when he could go back to Archie's and I had to keep putting him off. Unfortunately, his attendance at the motor traders was getting worse and he was on the verge of getting the sack until the day I went to meet him and he was sacked for refusing to tidy up after a delivery. I suppose he never learnt to do any tidying with Archie and he wasn't going to start somewhere he didn't want to be.

Kevin was taken off work experience after that. The last I heard he was refusing to do anything, staying in his bedroom all day. As far as he was concerned, he'd had his best chance at life. What was there to live for?

Well, that's the thing. Archie is still there, I go and see him from time to time. Still scruffy and unkempt but mowed under with work. He's even repaired my wife's pick-up truck after it collided with a pheasant. He did a brilliant job.

I mused about the effect Archie had on me and his attitude to life. He had made me yearn to go back and talk to my father, to help him have more resolve. Dad was a victim of his circumstances and he also thought his chances in life had gone. I would have told him that it doesn't matter what the opportunity is, you should still take them as you have no idea where they will lead. Life doesn't end at the first hurdle. But I also know that he wouldn't have listened to me, just like Kevin won't listen to me now and he's only 15.

Although unlike Kevin, my father had an unshakeable faith in education.

"You see, lad," he would say. "All the clever bastards in this world, the ones screwing the working man to the ground, the lawyers, accountants, bankers and politicians. They all took their O-levels and went to university." He would pause and drop his head forward-looking at the floor clasping his hands. He was the shell of the man he used to be. Tears welled up in his eyes. "If you don't want to be fucked up like me then get an education and get the fuck out of here." He pointed at an imaginary world beyond the walls of the house.

They were wise words that I couldn't ignore so I passed my exams and went to university and my other experiences also taught me how to climb the social ladder. My approach may have resembled that of a brawler in a cheap bar but as with any fight, by the end, you want to be the last man standing. I may no longer resemble the enthusiastic youth I once was but if you can pick yourself up, dust yourself down and still believe in yourself then you never know what may be around the corner.

Let It Snow

Ibra was sitting slumped in his chair. It was one of those days when everything that can go wrong had gone wrong. One of his students had been sacked, another hadn't turned up for work and he had just come off the phone from a lecture by a potential employer who said that some of the younger generations didn't have the same level of resilience he had when he was young, so there was no chance he would have a student on work experience.

"No chance." Ibra sighed. "What was it like for him when he started out?" He didn't wait for me to answer. "He said the student would bugger off or break something. I'm never going to get this lass a placement."

5 more minutes passed while Ibra brooded over his failure, his mood darkening, his body sliding even further down his chair. Then his phone rang. He turned it over in his fingers to read the screen and after what seemed like an eternity and put it to his ear.

"Hello, Ibra speaking."

"Oh yeah, mmm," he said.

"Yup. Yup, mmm," he continued.

"OK. Brilliant. Bye!" He pressed the button to end the call.

"Get in! I've still got it!" he exclaimed.

"Got what?" I asked.

"The magic man!" he said. He unfolded himself, sprang up like a jack in the box and began pacing around the room.

"I knew I'd get a placement for her. Interview tomorrow!" His shoulders were pumping like a championship boxer.

"Well done, you lucky bugger!" I said.

"Luck! Luck?" he exclaimed, a big smile spreading across his face. "This ain't luck boy, it's skill."

"It reminds me of something," I said.

"Oh yeah, such as?"

"When I was looking for work when I was a kid," I continued.

"I didn't have to bother, mum and dad were loaded," he said almost matter-of-factly. "My first job was in a shoe shop while I was at university. I was 22."

"I was 14," I said. "I delivered the local free paper for 1p per paper."

"How much? That's daylight robbery. Even Dick Turpin wore a cape," he replied.

"I'm glad you're back on form mate but this was 1984," I said. "I took delivery of 900 papers each Wednesday and was expected to deliver them by Thursday evening. The only way I could achieve that was to draft in the help of my brother. Between us, we just about managed the job by working three shifts; Wednesday night, Thursday morning, before school and Thursday night. 450 papers across 3 shifts each, 150 papers per shift weighing approx. 15–20kg each time!"

"Man alive. So you had to split the money with your kid brother?" Ibra asked.

"Sure did," I said. "Because the first time I tried, I couldn't get all the papers in the bag at once. It was like a sack of concrete."

Ibra laughed. He'd certainly got over his bout of depression. "But what's this got to do with my new placement?" he asked.

"Resilience, Ibra," I replied. "When against the odds, you dig in and keep going. That's what it was for you to get the placement for that girl and for me delivering 450 newspapers."

He rolled his eyes. I could see he was thinking, "not another lecture" but I carried on anyway. I began to describe how my Thursday night shift was the hardest of the 3. I explained that I had to walk a mile to the top estate with a full bag of newspapers before I could even begin. I then had the gruelling task of bending down to deliver the paper before struggling upright again so I could carry on to the next property. Each repetition being worth 1p.

"Sounds horrendous," said Ibra and added. "But getting a placement is harder!"

"Behave, there were 120 houses!" I replied.

"£1.20," calculated Ibra. "It wouldn't buy a sandwich these days."

"Exactly and it took nearly 3 hours. How long did that phone call take, 30 seconds? That wasn't the end of it either," I continued. "I then had to travel even further from home to deliver to the bigger, posher houses and there were another 30 of those."

"Oh yeah," he said. "You win. Carry on. No pun intended!"

"Well," I said, "I remember this particular day I was listening to my Walkman and I remember clearly listening to one of my sister's cassettes."

"Walkman?" he queried.

"The Sony Walkman," I said wistfully, "the smartphone of the '80s. It meant you could listen to music on the go. It made the paper-round more bearable."

I continued. "Anyway, I absent-mindedly stepped inside this driveway while I was listening to Wham's *Make It Big*. I had the paper in my hand and I was looking for the letterbox."

Ibra was mouthing the words to Wham songs. I was convinced it was *Last Christmas* because I'm certain that's the only one he knows.

"Just then and without any warning, a large Alsatian dog shot from the undergrowth barking its head off." I mimicked the dog barking, snapping Ibra out of his revelry.

"You scared me then!" he said.

"Just like me," I said, "it scared me shitless. I was so scared that I dropped the paper and ran for the gate. I could see that I wasn't going to get through it in time so I jumped for it and half landed, half fell on top of it, with the bag and one leg on the driveway and the rest of me outside the property."

"Go on," he said with a grin.

"Well, by now, George Michael had slipped off my head and the cassette had spilt out of the Walkman," I continued. "Fortunately, it was on the pavement and not on the driveway. Unfortunately, the dog had caught up with me and was ragging the bottom of my jeans, so I kicked and spluttered until it let go."

"What happened then?" he asked.

"Two things," I replied. "Firstly, the dog wandered back to where it had come from and started ragging the paper I had dropped and secondly, the owner came out."

"Did he say anything?" asked Ibra.

"First off, he was angry," I replied. "He called the dog off and asked in less than a polite way what I was doing."

"So what did you say?"

"That I was delivering the paper and waved one in the air to show him."

"Seems reasonable to me," he mused. "What was his problem?"

"I was so lost in the music I hadn't read the sign that said 'Beware of the dog'. I was supposed to use a side entrance," I replied.

"So? His dog had given you a rough time. You could sue! What did he say then?"

"This was 1984, Ibra, he just told me to push off and take my crappy paper with me. I felt a complete idiot."

"Man, what a prat," he declared. "Anyway, it seems to me there's more than one lesson in this, Charlie."

"Oh yeah, what's that?"

"Well, resilience is one thing but not paying attention is the other. It can drop you right in it!" He laughed at his own joke. "Right I'm off," he said.

"Now you beware of the dog!" I quipped as he left the room.

The thing is I continued with that job, rain or shine because it was my ticket to avoid the ticket; the free school meal ticket. I didn't want to discuss this with Ibra because there's still a sense of shame in having been on free school meals.

At school, they gave kids who were on free school meals yellow tickets to 'pay' for the meals. We had to queue on the left-hand side of the hall while everyone else queued on the right. This gave the other kids ample opportunity to take the mickey out of us and make us feel small. For the life of me, I could never work out whether the school engineered this ritual humiliation or whether it was a simple accident. It was certainly symptomatic of a time when society was less tolerant of peoples' differences.

So I used the money I earned to pay for my school meals and avoid this humiliation. I was earning £4.50 a week and my school meals were 60p a time, leaving me with £2.10; the price of 3x60 minute cassettes, 2 chart singles or halfway to the cost of a pair of jeans, if I was lucky.

At the time my dad, although very opinionated about what jobs he was prepared to do, was happy to exploit the fact I wasn't. He would ask to borrow from me all the time but borrow didn't necessarily mean I would get it back. £4.50 was a day's drinking. Approximately, 10 pints of Yorkshire bitter, unless you bought cigarettes and took a taxi to the pub, in which case £4.50 stretched to about half a day's drinking and some smokes. When the unemployment giro came through, I would feel terrible asking for the money back. My dad didn't necessarily tell my mum he'd borrowed off me so when she went to the post office to cash the giro, I would keep quiet and resolve myself to try and earn more and keep clear of dad on payday.

Sad though it may seem, my dad owed me £80 when he died, equivalent to about 175 pints of Tetley Bitter in the Top End club.

My conversation with Ibra led to more thoughts about the past. Ibra would be well on his way to his next visit but I had the luxury of a bit of time to myself and it led me to ponder how my career took an unexpected turn due to a visit from the free paper agent, the man who dropped the papers off at my house, ready for me to deliver the next day. He suddenly appeared at our front door one Friday afternoon which was not the normal day for papers and asked my mum if he could take me out for half an hour for a chat. Puzzled, my mum said it was OK and we set off in his car in silence. We drove approximately 2 miles when he stopped abruptly at the end of a track that led into fields.

"Get out," he said and I opened the door with hesitation.

"Follow me," he continued and set off down the track.

I trotted along behind him completely lost as to what he was going to do. As we walked, the car got further behind us and just as it disappeared out of sight he stopped and turned towards me, pointing into the undergrowth.

"In there," he snapped. My mind was racing, I'd heard about people like him so I was about to run as fast as I could, as far away from the old pervert as possible.

"In there," he repeated. "In there"—he stuttered—"is a pile of papers; a pile of papers that I believe you should have delivered over the last month."

"What?" I spluttered in relief.

"Papers. Dumped!" he shouted.

"Calm down," I replied. "I don't know what you're talking about," gathering my composure.

"You don't, eh? Well, let me tell you something, young man. The paper company put a stamp on each paper identifying which paper boy is to deliver the paper and these have got your mark on them. You've dumped them," he said.

I took a little time to think things through and he took this as a sign that he'd caught his culprit.

"Got nothing to say?" he asked. A look of satisfaction was on his face. The man was an idiot.

My response wasn't as calm as I would have liked but I made my point. Firstly, we didn't have a car, so shifting 4,000 papers to this spot had to be done by hand. Bearing in mind the site was 2 miles from home, then my brother and I would have to walk 4 miles to dump each batch and it would take us 3 visits, so 12 miles for the last 4 weeks to dump the papers; it therefore made no sense for us to dump them, moreover it made much more sense to deliver them as agreed.

Secondly, the special mark was one of those new-fangled barcodes found on every paper. It was on the papers I had at home the previous day. Why a free paper had a barcode was beyond me but it was the reason why I thought he was an idiot. I didn't say that last bit to him, just in case he was a pervert.

He just looked at me. "Right," he said, "so it wasn't you then?"

I just looked at him.

He stared back and without a word, turned around towards the car and eventually reaching it, he took me home. I resolved to find another job as soon as I could. Trust can easily be lost and I no longer had trust in this man whatsoever. Where the hell did he get his theory from?

I learnt my third valuable lesson on that job and that's about trust and being able to stand up for yourself in the right way. I knew I had to stay calm and stick to the facts. It would have been so easy for me to tell the guy to f-off and walk away. I was, after all, 15 and that would have been an acceptable response from a young lad whose emotions were revolving like a 1,400 spin washing machine. But I had my own self-esteem to consider, I knew I had to stand my ground and tell the truth.

Unfortunately, so many of my students struggle to grasp what standing on their own two feet is but I was learning from them that there were numerous reasons for that.

This has left some young people incapable of stepping comfortably into adulthood. Either they haven't been taught the skills, been given the boundaries or they've spent years being protected from themselves and the rest of the world. It is now a huge leap for some of them.

It is also important to acknowledge that neither do they have the opportunities that I did to start working at a young age, partly due to overbearing parenting but also because there are so many cheap distractions that are so easy to access, things that cost me so much more in time and money back in the 1980s. Even something as basic as music which is pretty much free these days, cost an arm and a leg back then. Young people can now get lost in a virtual world for next to nothing and some parents are happy for them to exist in that world as there is a belief it keeps them out of trouble.

And it's not just the kids. Many of the parents I work with struggle due to cheap distractions. They struggle to keep away from alcohol and they dabble with drugs. It's a spiralling circle of victimhood and sidestepping responsibility that has a low financial threshold. It is certainly not a new thing but 24-hour TV, social media and the sheer price of them allow people to remain disengaged from society.

This is why I do my job. It is in the hope that I can break the cycle in a similar fashion that I did when I was a young person. Fortunately, by using my experiences as examples, I can help break that cycle in a good number of cases because people are curious and like to identify with familiar struggles. Some students, along with their own resolve and newfound resilience, follow the advice and tend to grasp their opportunities and go on to contribute to society. Often this takes time and effort to get going and relies on everyone not giving in at the first sign of resistance. Again, I fall back on my own experiences when confronted with resistance. I remind myself of the times I'd struggle trying to start one of the old cars I drove around in the 1980s. Inevitably it would be on the worst day in the worst weather. The car would prove to be reliable in its unreliability but when I did manage to get it going, the relief was palpable as it often kept going and got me to my destination. Not that I think any of my students are old bangers but the relief when they engage in work experience is like nectar to a bee.

My next job was as a silver service waiter at an upmarket pub. My uniform was a white shirt, dark trousers and a black bow tie. For a 15-year-old council house lad, this was a leap into the unknown but at £1 an hour and eight hours a week plus tips, I had doubled my wages from delivering papers. It was hard work. I managed 2 years and it paid for all sorts of things to keep me up to date with the latest fashions.

I had, however, set my heights higher than waitering and I wanted to buy a car so I took a job working for a DIY store. The issue of the lack of transport became immediately apparent as my shift began at 9 am on a Sunday morning and the buses didn't run early enough to get me there on time.

Therefore, I had to walk the 3 miles to work, setting off at 8 am so I wasn't late. I didn't care, I was earning a proper wage and it didn't matter how frustrated people got, or how angry the customers might become, I took it all in my stride. I'd heard it all before, particularly working as a waiter. I really enjoyed that job, it wasn't a career choice but it could have been if I had wanted it. However, I had my sights set on getting to university like I had promised my dad. I was in the final year of my A-levels and therefore, I didn't want to give up at such a late stage. One other benefit to working at the DIY store was that I was paid directly into my bank account rather than being paid in cash. This way my money was safe from dad and I could therefore save the majority of it for a motor. It took me 2 years.

My first car was a pile of crap, the one that would never start. It was an electric blue Austin Allegro with a 1300 petrol engine. It was so uncool that it was – cool. It had a hole in the floor behind the driver's seat, so if I took passengers they had to be careful climbing in the back. It rattled when you went above 60 miles an hour and used more oil than petrol. The thing is I had no one who could advise me on a car as we had never had one in our family and no one could drive, therefore, I bought the first one I saw with my £500 budget. A car bought for £500 today would be infinitely better than my Austin Allegro and that's after 25+ years of inflation!

Once more, the contrast with modern life is stark. Firstly, the MOT applied to cars back then was regularly circumvented with garage owners waving through death traps on a daily basis. The dealer selling my car clearly saw me coming and made a killing, well nearly. These days the dealer would have been fined heavily for selling such a death trap and I am amazed to this day that it lasted over 2 years before it eventually blew its head gasket and died. If you're interested, I then fell in love with another pile of rust without thinking. A Talbot Solara. I realise that most people have probably never heard of one and there's a reason. They were crap as well. My car history is therefore one of failed love affairs over many years.

However, they gave me my mobility and I used my car whenever I could afford to put petrol in it. One key appointment I always made was to help mum with the weekly shopping. I would pick her up from outside the dental practice where she worked part-time as a dental nurse. We would then drive the short distance to the supermarket, where she would do her shopping before we'd have lunch in the supermarket cafe and then drive home.

On one occasion after shopping, we went to the cafe to find it had been upgraded. Gone were the individual wooden tables and chairs, glass pepper-pots and ceramic crockery and in came fully moulded tables, with the chairs attached directly to the legs so you couldn't move the position of the chair. You had to slide yourself in like climbing into the cockpit of a rocket. No longer was it a tea shop, it was more like a set from *2000: A Space Odyssey.*

We hung the shopping bags onto one of the table chairs that were next to each other and went to select our sandwiches. When we returned, we squeezed in next to each other so we could look out of the window while we chatted. However, just as we were placing our posteriors on the seat, the whole table tilted backwards as it pivoted on its legs, and half trapped in the seat we couldn't stop it. We ended up on our backs facing the ceiling, trapping the shopping beneath us, with our legs in the air staring at the moulded seats that were attached to the opposite side of the table. To compound the embarrassment, the sandwiches were scattered all over our faces and there was a pool of tea on the floor. We were completely trapped. All we could do was look at each other and laugh. It was a ridiculous situation to be in. After what felt like an eternity, we were helped in extracting ourselves from the plastic trap. And, once the laughing had subsided, we cleaned ourselves up and left as hastily as we could, burdened with the shopping and smelling faintly of tinned salmon sandwiches.

What these tales offer are opportunities to learn something about ourselves and the society we live in. Sometimes it is the fact that an upgrade isn't necessarily an improvement, or that doing a job properly isn't necessarily appreciated like it should be.

However, if Ibra had still been in the office, we would have at least been able to answer the question as to whether we are more or less resilient now than we were.

Back then, I was extremely embarrassed by some of the situations I ended up in but at no time did it occur to me to blame anyone but myself.

Now it's a different story.

If I was in the same circumstances today as I was then, instead of laughing it off or feeling embarrassed, I'd be far more inclined to feign my injuries and sue their backsides off the tea shop for negligence.

I'd Like to Teach the World to Sing

The surroundings were a little different to what I normally expected. There was a neat little garden surrounded by ornately painted railings. A large front door covered in fresh paint and polished brass furniture, a door bell which rang clear and was answered immediately. The sky was grey with clouds and a typical winter chill was in the air as it was only 2 weeks to Christmas.

"Come in," said Mrs Hunter. "We've been expecting you."

She was smiling broadly and was clutching a little Yorkshire Terrier. "This is Buddy, I hope you like dogs?"

Buddy looked at me with friendly eyes. All I could think was, put the bloody thing down! But she was holding him very firmly.

"Yes," I lied; I was getting good at it. We'd had a Yorkshire Terrier when I was a child. My dad called it 'The Rat'. It was appropriate.

She nodded politely to a door on the right of the corridor and I proceeded through to a well-lit room filled with a collection of vintage furniture including sideboards, leather sofas, easy chairs and cabinets full of highly collectable items from pocket watches to small delicately fired porcelain figurines.

Everything was neatly placed, meticulously clean and positioned with care. This was what I envisaged was bohemian style. There was also a Christmas tree made up of tinsel and homemade baubles.

"Do you like the tree?" she asked.

"Yes, it's lovely," I replied thinking that having a Christmas tree decorated with as much care as a child's sticker book was one of the strangest customs of the western world.

"Would you like a drink?" she said politely.

"No, thank you," I replied. This was standard policy. I don't accept any hospitality from my clients just in case I caught some horrific condition, although in this case, I considered I was pretty safe.

"Well if you don't mind, I'll have one," she said and off she scuttled to the kitchen. The next thing I heard was a scurrying of little feet and without much warning, the Yorkshire Terrier shot into the living room as I was just settling onto a large Chesterfield sofa. It jumped from a good 3 feet away and landed squarely on my lap.

"Buddy!" cried Mrs Hunter. "Buddy, come here!"

She walked into the living room. "Get down, Buddy," she squawked. "Lickle, Buddy, Wuddy." Buddy just flattened his ears and dug his nails into my legs.

"Sorry about that, he's just very affectionate, aren't you Buddy?" she said.

"It's OK," I lied again and with that, she went back to the kitchen. Over the next 2 minutes, it was a battle between dog and man; me increasingly becoming frustrated with my attempts to keep the dog off my lap and Buddy finding the whole thing a huge game. Just as I pushed him off for the 4th time and Buddy landed with an audible thump, Mrs Hunter re-entered the room with a tray and gave me a long stare.

"I brought you a cup just in case," she said, brushing aside her obvious disapproval.

"Thank you, but I'm OK," I said. I was relieved to be rid of the dog because as soon as Mrs Hunter sat down, Buddy shot across the room to sit on her lap instead.

"Milk?" she insisted.

"No, thank you. I'm fine," I replied with frustration, unsure whether she had actually taken any notice of what I had said. After a while, I asked her quite simply, "Where is Bethany?"

"Oh, I'll go get her in a minute, I just want to give her a few moments to compose herself before you meet her," she said.

"OK," I replied with uncertainty. "Is there anything I can help you with?"

"Possibly," she mused and stirred the tea with care. This drew my attention to her hands which were expertly manicured and dripping with jewellery.

"Beth is very delicate at the moment, so I have to take care with what I say to her and also how I say it." With that, she carefully placed Buddy on the floor and left the room leaving myself and the dog alone to resume our tag wrestling game. He won.

A few moments later, she returned with Bethany in tow. She was no more than 5' 2" tall, with extremely long hair that hung in a ragged mess over her face. A face that was puffy from sleep, with eyes screwed up into a tight knot to avoid the light that was streaming in through the high windows. She had delicate hands and feet and was wearing very little apart from an oversized cropped vest top and black cropped shorts. The only other item was her mobile phone, clutched tightly in her hands, typical of the modern teenager. Clearly, Bethany had spent little time composing herself and more time messaging on her phone and pressing the snooze button; she was nearly naked.

Mrs Hunter ignored the tangled mess that was her daughter, almost as if she would ignore a brawl on the other side of the street or ignore a tramp asleep in the doorway of Harrods. Instead, she offered me tea which I reluctantly accepted and took care in placing it on the side table, as the dog was still balanced precariously upon my lap. Once Bethany had settled on one of the sofas and curled up into a ball with a cushion over her head, Buddy removed himself from my jeans and went to lie with her.

Mrs Hunter drew a large breath and composed herself before she spoke, "Bethany dear, this is Charlie, he would like to speak with you about undertaking work experience." Her voice was like double cream pouring over freshly picked strawberries.

In reply, there was a muffled tweet from underneath the cushion. "I know who it is."

"Good," replied her mum. "Would you be so kind as to pay both him and me your full attention?"

Bethany began to uncurl herself from the foetal position and push the long strands of webbed hair from her face. Underneath was a pleasant-looking young girl who had very sparkling, happy eyes. However, each time her mum spoke to her, her eyes would glaze over like a cataract.

"How are you?" I asked.

"Fine, thanks." She smiled, making her eyes sparkle even more. I could see there was more to Bethany than initially meets the eye. Her mum sat quietly by. She looked unsure as to what to expect.

"Have you considered what kind of work experience you want?" I asked.

"Not sure actually, maybe something to do with hair?" With that, she looked across at her mum. Mrs Hunter was facing her with what now seemed like sympathy on her face but said nothing.

"I know a brilliant hairdresser called Tina that would be a very good fit," I said, hoping she would show more interest.

Bethany suddenly showed alarm. "How old are they? Would I know anyone from school who would come in for their hair cutting?" She glanced at her phone with an expectation like someone might be listening.

"I don't know," I replied, a bit taken aback and looked at her mum.

"I can't go if anyone from school will be there," she said, becoming more agitated.

I tried reassuring her as much as I could. "It's all right, Bethany, for starters you will do work experience during school hours and secondly, their customers tend to be retired."

"You'll be fine, Beth," said Mrs Hunter as a follow-up.

"But I won't know anyone," wailed Bethany offering the complete opposite argument, her eyes now glazing over. "What if they don't want someone like me there? What if I make a mistake? It might be too far away."

"It will be fine, sweetheart," mum replied and with that, Buddy felt his best option was to return to my lap and jumped from Bethany's side onto the floor and across to me. He sat there stock still, shaking slightly. I thought it best to intervene.

"Bethany, this is a really good placement, they are fantastic people. Tina and Tracey have worked with lots of other girls I refer to them. They take a lot of time to settle people in, and they even have a training head so you can practice on that first."

"But it's happened so fast, I'm not ready to go to work," she wailed even more, her eyes now brimming with tears. The phone had been thrown into the folds of the sofa in frustration. We had gone from a relatively calm situation to a level of high anxiety in seconds and Bethany's imagination was creating barriers to avoid having to step out of the house and face the world.

"How are your sleeping patterns?" I asked, trying to divert her attention.

"They're terrible," replied Mrs Hunter. "She stays up late until 3 or 4 in the morning and then sleeps fitfully through the day."

"What about school?" I asked.

"I haven't been for weeks," sobbed Bethany. "I can't face going, with everyone looking at me, that's why I can't sleep. I'm getting so far behind."

"I bet your mealtimes and what you eat is affected as well?" I asked with confidence. "Is it mainly junk food, crisps, chocolate, anything other than a properly balanced meal?" I asked. She nodded in agreement.

"What triggered you to stop attending school?" I was really digging now to try and get to the bottom of Bethany's anxiety. Bethany had calmed down a little but didn't respond immediately and it was her mum that replied.

"Beth had a taster day at college for a hair and beauty course that would be starting in September. As part of the lesson, she was selected to do a demonstration with one of the teachers which included the removal of all Beth's makeup so they could show the other students how to build your makeup more professionally."

"What did you have to tell him that for?" She sobbed. "I didn't know they were going to do it, I felt stupid without my makeup."

"Beth ran out of the class and never went back, I think the school are hoping work experience would be a better option than college," said Mrs Hunter.

Having absorbed the exchange, I felt we needed to bring the meeting to a close and try another tack.

"I know this may seem odd coming from me but I understand that teenage girls these days think a lot about their makeup. Social media is awash with the perfect face and perfect way of presenting yourself; it's almost akin to being naked by not having any makeup on."

They both looked embarrassed. I felt the heat rise on the back of my neck and the cheeks on my face. I was wondering myself what I was going to say next.

"There were boys in the class, weren't there, Beth?" blurted Mrs Hunter before I could speak again.

"Shut up!" retorted Bethany, starting to show some interest in what I had to say. Buddy, who seemed to be a rather sensitive dog, just sat there shaking.

"Have you got girls?" Mrs Hunter asked.

"One but she's only 5. What I would say though is that she is really influenced by what she sees on the internet and is showing a lot of interest in makeup."

She raised her eyebrows and sat back. I was starting to notice that both Mrs Hunter and daughter had very distinct eyebrows, drawn and reshaped like you would a piece of plasticine.

"I can imagine, Bethany, that you spend a lot of time on social media when you're staying up late." She nodded.

"Well, for one thing, losing sleep and a bad diet does nothing for your skin or hair."

Both of them absent-mindedly took strands of their hair and examined them carefully. I had no idea if it was true but playing to their vanity was working.

"My advice," I continued, "is that you try and get into a better routine before we look at work experience." Bethany was settling down again now and showing some interest. As the energy levels were dropping, Buddy stopped shaking and went back across to Bethany. I asked my next question, almost knowing the answer.

"Do you go to the gym, Mrs Hunter?" I could sense her sit up a bit straighter before she then crossed her legs.

"I do actually," which she said in a way in which I had no doubt, was fishing for a complement.

"I didn't really need to ask," I replied leaning forward with a false smile. "But I think part of the routine that Bethany needs to get into is to go out more, and she could achieve that by going to the gym with you."

They both looked at each other and Mrs Hunter was obviously sceptical. I guessed her gym trips were part of an elaborate daily routine that also involved coffee and long lunches. I wasn't sure she would want Bethany tagging along. However, I persisted.

"I suggest that Bethany aims to eat with you at the proper mealtimes, goes to the gym, walks the dog and aims to try and get tired so that she actually wants to sleep. What do you think, Beth?"

"I'd really like that," she said looking at her mum, "but what if there's anyone I know at the gym?"

"You'll be fine, Beth," said mum obviously resigned to having to share her treasured routine, as Bethany's energy started to rise again. "I go around 10 o'clock so there will only be you and I." And a few other mums in the latest yoga pants, I thought.

I stood up before Buddy could make a dash for my lap again.

"OK then," said Bethany. "I'd like to try."

"Good," I said with relief as Buddy settled into Bethany's lap again. "The plan is we try and establish a better routine and then once we've made progress with that then I'll come back and organise a meeting with Tina at her salon. I'll be back after Christmas."

They both nodded and I left without even taking a sip of my tea.

Christmas passed quickly. Myself and my family took turns spending one or two days in bed with a stomach bug which the younger ones had brought home from school on the last day. Still, by the first week in January, we were all recovered and ready to return to school. I arranged to meet with Mrs Hunter and her daughter again and the changes were remarkable.

"You look really well," I said with conviction. Bethany was sitting upright, fully dressed in leggings and a hoody. Her hair was in a ponytail allowing her full visage to be on show.

Her makeup had been applied carefully, though apparently with a trowel, which was the style of the moment. Her eyebrows were manicured but shaped with a much larger arch, giving her a look of perpetual surprise. And she smiled, pleased with my compliment.

"I've organised for us to go and meet with Tina and Tracey tomorrow and it seems to me you are more than ready for it," I said.

"She is," said Mrs Hunter, pleased with herself. "She's been to the gym a few times, walked the dog and helped me prepare a few meals." A huge grin suddenly crossed her face and she sat back in satisfaction, turning away slightly as Buddy sat with her wagging his tail.

Bethany also looked pleased with herself, there was an obvious improvement in her well-being and she smiled so her eyes sparkled once more. If only she could tone down the makeup, I thought to myself. When college had picked her out on the taster day, they could see what I could see now but Bethany didn't have the confidence to see through their experiment.

"I'm looking forward to it," she said, like a child not sure what a trip to Disney World was like but looking forward to it all the same.

"That's brilliant," I replied. "I'll pick you up tomorrow at 10 o'clock and we'll go together to the salon."

The next day I was there on time and Bethany was ready and waiting for me, dressed simply in cropped jeans and trainers, and also wearing a couple of hoodies instead of a coat. She was clutching her phone tightly like a hand grenade. The previous day's confidence was still apparent and this had rubbed off on me, so I was also in an ebullient mood.

Tina and Tracey can only be described as fabulous. They cut and styled the hair of most of the retired ladies in the Scargyll area of town. Both of them had teenage daughters so they understood the histrionics that went with stroppy young teenagers and dealt with it sympathetically. They were also incredibly helpful, tactful and supportive.

Entering the salon was through the front door of an everyday terrace house, down a typical garden path. Once in the white painted corridor, you entered the cutting room through a plain door to the left. The tall Victorian window fed copious amounts of light into the room which had 3 cutting chairs, 2 drying stations, a hair washing station and 3 chairs set back into the bay window as a waiting area.

"Morning!" They sang. "Who's this then?" they asked.

"It's Bethany," I replied.

"So you want to come here to do work experience?" Tina asked Bethany, who was suddenly feeling their direct attention with discomfort.

"Yes, please," she said, barely audibly, her phone passing between her hands like a bar of soap. Tina and Tracey continued to cut their respective customer's hair, both of whom were having their curls trimmed while sipping coffee.

"So, you like doing your hair then?" Tracey added. Bethany nodded with a thin smile, the phone slipping back and forth between her fingers. I imagined it squirting out and flying across the room like a torpedo into one of the sinks.

"OK then," said Tina, "let's see how you get on tomorrow. We'll see you at 9 o'clock."

We both said our goodbyes and left the way we came. It was short and sweet but they both knew Bethany would be nervous and kept it that way deliberately.

"How did you find that?" I asked Bethany with some reservation.

"OK," she replied a little distantly, my confidence evaporating quicker than our breath in the cold January air.

"Are you still OK for tomorrow?" I pressed a little, needing reassurance. She turned and smiled but her eyes were distant.

"Sure," she said and with that, I took her back home.

I returned the next day before 9 am to make sure we would be there on time. Mrs Hunter answered the door and ushered me inside.

"She won't go," she said simply.

"Why not?" I asked.

"Ask her yourself," she replied as we entered the brightly lit living room.

Bethany was lying on the sofa in a similar pose to the first time I saw her. I didn't wait for her to acknowledge me, I just got straight down to it.

"Why won't you go, Beth?"

She hesitated as she turned over towards me. Her hair was once again a tangled mess and she was hugging her phone for comfort.

"I can't," she said eventually. "They'll think I'm stupid."

There was another pause. I felt it best to keep quiet as she considered her next argument.

"What if I make a mistake? What if someone I know comes in? I just can't do it!"

Mrs Hunter was starting to get frustrated with her.

"I know what's wrong with you, that boyfriend of yours has been around while I've been out, hasn't he?"

That was unexpected! If there was a time to just keep out of an argument, this was it.

"Yeah, so what!" shouted Bethany. "Doesn't mean I can go to the hairdressers."

"Doesn't mean you can't either," replied Mrs Hunter. "Lying in bed all day and night with him is no way to prepare for your first day. When you're not with him, you're constantly messaging him."

"I was scared. I was looking for some comfort," she sobbed. "You don't understand what it's like!"

"What you need is a reality check young lady," said Mrs Hunter. She had made her mind up to manage her daughter in a completely different fashion. Gone was the sympathy and understanding, I had the impression Mrs Hunter had seen through her daughter's facade and was putting some steel into her approach. Bethany didn't reply. Now was the time for me to step in.

"Bethany," I said quietly. "Having anxieties about starting something new is normal. It is not unique to you, everyone feels the same thing. The big difference is there are those who can overcome those anxieties without creating unnecessary barriers." She was sobbing quietly. I continued regardless.

"Imagine going to Blackpool Pleasure Beach," I said. Both women looked at me now, wondering where I was going next. I continued, "And you'd heard that there was a ride that was both exhilarating and frightening. One of those bucket list rides you just have to do."

I had their attention now.

"I think the one you mean is the Pepsi Max," said Bethany.

"Yes, that's the one," I acknowledged. "Anyway, you get there and although you're worried about the Pepsi Max, you join the queue. However, it's a long queue and as you wait, you become more apprehensive as time passes by. You start to imagine bad things will happen like falling off, or the ride coming to a halt at its maximum height, something like that."

They were both completely absorbed by my story.

"So you still queue and eventually, you get to the front and are asked to get in. At this point, you have a choice, get in or step across and bottle it. However, you've painted the perfect disaster in your head and you decide that you can't get on the ride; you're rigid with fear so you cross over. But as you step over, you notice those who've just been on the ride are smiling. You realise that for all the fear they had while they were queuing, they were exhilarated and happy and were sharing their experiences with one another."

I took a small breath and noticed the realisation on both their faces. I breathed out slowly and continued.

"Disappointed with yourself, you think that you'd like to try again but unfortunately, you've already lost your place in the car and so you're going to have to queue once more. But if you're ever going to get that feeling of achievement, you're going to have to do it. Do you understand what I mean?" They both nodded. "You've got to try and go to work tomorrow if you can't overcome your fear today."

Bethany had stopped crying and her mum was lost for words.

"I'll go back to Tina's and see what they say about a start tomorrow instead."

With that, I went to see them and with typical intuitive advice, they suggested Bethany made her own way to work rather than me bringing her. They wanted Bethany to show commitment to working at Tina's and when I told Mrs Hunter about their response, she said she would make sure Beth would go to work the next day.

And so with apprehension, I had waited until late the next morning before I rang Mrs Hunter to ask how things had gone with Bethany.

"Fine," she said with aplomb. "I rang Tina and Beth loves it. She's riding the Pepsi Max!"

"That's fantastic!" I replied. "I'm glad my advice worked."

"Yes it worked," she said. "But I had to threaten to cancel her mobile phone contract to get her on the damned thing!"

Don't Leave Me This Way

Consider Special Forces soldiers armed to the teeth, bursting through a door to attack an enemy. Each decision made is a calculated risk based on their combat skills, training, weaponry and the manpower behind them. They make their move because the odds are in their favour and therefore, the prospect of death is greatly reduced. Well, not their deaths anyway. But that's still the choice, a choice between life and death. Maybe you turn left away from trouble or you turn right. You keep to the path or you step off the cliff, you burst through the door or throw a hand-grenade in first.

The young people I work with generally turn right, step off the cliff or burst through the door without considering the consequences. This often leads to a life of perpetual frustration and constant bouncing from one crisis to another. In these circumstances, schools are left with only one choice when a student constantly rails against the system and does not comply with expectations, and that is to exclude them permanently. More often than not, my involvement comes when the head teacher has a twitchy finger on the trigger of the exclusion gun. My job is to try and stop them from pulling it.

Take young Gareth Bilson, at 14 years old he had a normal life, living in the calm waters that lay way ahead of a crisis. Then one day, out of the blue, his dad goes to work and doesn't come home and suddenly great waves rush in and wash him overboard. This creates a crisis because his dad is not dead; he just decides to live somewhere else with someone else and not Gareth. And when Gareth and his mum realise what has happened, they are thrown into turmoil.

If his dad had died, then things would have been different. Under those circumstances, we have a choice either to get on with life or not. I understand this choice and I have seen the effects that a parent dying can have on people when they are young.

In my own case, the period before my dad died was a crisis. There was a constant stream of decisions and actions that kept everyone floating around in the flotsam of a shipwreck. Day after day, we simply existed, never being in a position to improve our prospects. Somehow, I managed to crawl onto a door that was floating by which opened up a better future for me. That door represented my willingness to work. But the real improvement in my prospects came when dad died. It is a sad fact but it sometimes only takes one person to affect the lives of so many others.

But Gareth was still stuck in a perpetual storm. His dad was making the most of his newfound relationship and didn't see him for months. His mum found solace in a bottle of wine each night, eventually crying herself to sleep and taking little heed of the household chores and the people in it. Therefore Gareth, faced with the example his parents were setting, decided he wouldn't follow the rules either.

It started with insolence in class, ignoring his teacher's requests to calm down and not be disruptive. It then began to escalate to the point where Gareth was regularly being asked to leave the room and sit on a chair in the corridor outside the classroom. This punishment was intended to be a purgatory of boredom but there were many other students like Gareth who had also been asked to leave the classroom due to their poor behaviour and this fostered new and interesting relationships that Gareth enjoyed. He kept on being disruptive so he could befriend the other kids in the corridor.

Mum was forever going to school to try and show willingness and attempt to improve Gareth's behaviour but she was now blaming Gareth for a lot of her ills and couldn't look him in the eye anymore. He was starting to be excluded on a regular basis which was putting his mum under pressure to supervise him during the day. She was often hung over and trying to keep her mobile nail bar business going at the same time. Gareth soon learned that his mum had little interest in him which meant he could leave the house for hours on end without her caring, and this is when the trouble escalated.

Buoyed by his newfound friendships, he began shoplifting to the consternation of the local high street shops. This gave him kudos with his cronies but he ended up with a restraining order excluding him from encroaching within 200 yards of the high street. His mum had now lost control and Gareth, without his father's interest too, took his stealing to another level.

One day walking along the road between home and school, he and a friend met another younger student. Gareth was only small with size 4 feet and the student coming towards him had the latest trainers on. They looked the right size, so Gareth produced a knife and demanded them. He put them on even though they were too big and laughing, carried on his way.

Gareth was now becoming a major problem at home, at school and in society. He had attracted the attention of the police and the family had now suffered the ignominy of the scrutiny of an intervention officer and social worker. It was quickly established by the intervention team that because of mum's declining mental health, dad must be forced to re-enter Gareth's life and establish some boundaries and that Gareth must also engage with alternatives to the academic curriculum, namely work experience. The stage was set for me to enter his life and try and prevent a predictable, dramatic failure.

I met with his social worker Shelly one wet Monday morning at the beginning of December. It had taken Gareth 4 months to descend to the point where engagement was essential, otherwise, he would be permanently excluded from school.

The meeting took place at a nondescript building built some time in the 1970s. Constructed of cheap red bricks in block fashion, it had large windows and deep wooden soffits with a flat roof. I had to ring to enter the building and was received with suspicion by a sour-faced receptionist who ushered me into the building and I was encouraged to follow her through a large open-plan office hushed with concerned and concentrated faces. No one was distracted by my presence. I didn't expect a fire eater or juggling act to welcome me but they were deliberately ignoring me for reasons I couldn't fathom at that moment. I was then asked to wait in the smallest room you could possibly fit 4 people into.

You had to manoeuvre chairs so you could open the door and also to allow people to sit at the other side of the table. I sat waiting for 20 minutes.

Eventually, Shelly breezed into the room. She did not offer to shake my hand, make an apology for being late or offer me a drink. It was strictly business. I was taken aback if I'm honest. I understand that social workers will see things the rest of us would rather not but being so hardened to their jobs can make them dispassionate, aloof and if I'm frank, dislikeable. I've been in dozens of meetings with social workers and I'm afraid almost all of them are like this. They actively avoid revealing anything about themselves and therefore, their personality suffers. I firmly believe that if they could use a code name instead of their real name, they would. Not 007, more like 00, Oh no! Because that's what it's like to sit through a meeting with them.

Shelly was no different, she laid out the circumstances that Gareth was in, namely that he was now living with his dad but would be under the responsibility of his mum during school hours. This was because dad lived 10 miles out of town and school was only a mile from mum's home. She also explained that she expected me to find work experience for Gareth to form part of his rehabilitation. I politely pointed out that as much as she may have done a risk assessment on Gareth, it was my duty to meet him and his parents to carry out my own risk assessment and would get back to her as soon as I could. To my surprise, she then gathered her things and stood up and with reluctance she accepted my terms and left the room. All the while she kept talking, asking me to email her as soon as I had made progress, her voice dwindling as she walked away. She didn't return and I was left in the broom cupboard wondering what was going on.

I waited for her to return but another 20 minutes had passed before I eventually stuck my head around the door and waited to catch someone's eye. This becomes quite a difficult task when they're all actively trying to ignore you. A young lady eventually relented and showed me to the door, explaining that Shelly had had to leave at short notice due to a last-minute development in one of her cases. I found myself ushered outside, standing in the pouring rain. Charming!

I arranged to meet Sarah Bilson at her home which was at the end of a long row of small, terraced houses. Each frontage was neat and tidy and Sarah's was no different. I stepped straight into the living room from the street as she bustled me in. As soon as I sat down she started talking;

"You won't believe what he did last night," she said. "Went out wi' his mates, running around the old mill on Salts Street, sets fire to some rubbish and the Fire Brigade had to go and put it out. He got picked up by the police and was driven home to his dad's. Said it wasn't him but I know it was. There's no talkin' to ' im. He's also ridin' a bike I've never seen before, so I don't know where 'e got that from."

"Right," I replied. I didn't know what else to say.

"I don't think you've got a cat in hells chance of gettin' 'im into work experience. All it would take would be for someone to look at 'im funny and he'd be off."

Just then the door rattled as a key was put in the lock and it opened abruptly.

"What're you doin' 'ere?" she said. In walked Gareth, a small, young-looking boy. Immediately, I felt he was too young to be at work. He may be 15 now but his whole demeanour was one of a naughty school boy, rather than an aspiring adult.

"Got excluded," he said with a level of triumph I found disturbing.

"What for?" she screamed with despair.

"I'm not 'aving that bitch tell me to put me tie back on," he said and walked into the kitchen.

"Gareth!" She was talking to his back. "I've got an appointment in an hour. Why can't you just behave yourself? I can't take you everywhere wi' me, yer know." She turned back to face me.

"Fucking Hell!" she said through clenched teeth. "I can't leave him 'ere, I don't trust him. He'll steal summat and sell it for money."

"He doesn't look like the type," I said.

"Don't you be fooled; he's been a little bastard recently. He's drivin' me mad. I'm only just keepin' me 'ead above water."

"What's for dinner?" came a voice from the kitchen.

"What d' yer mean?" she replied. "You're not meant to be 'ere, so there's nowt for dinner, you should be 'aving your lunch at school."

"Fuck Sake!" came the reply.

"Don't talk to me like that, please," she said, missing the irony. Gareth didn't reply. Instead, he wandered into the room.

"I'm Charlie," I interjected. "I'm here to discuss with your mum the prospect of you doing work experience."

"I can do that," he replied, ignoring the previous exchange. "Done some plasterin' in 'ere wi' me dad." He pointed to the wall behind my head.

Mum nodded in agreement.

"That's useful," I replied. "Do you want to get into construction?"

"Nah," he dismissed my suggestion immediately. "I like cars. My dad's got a Vauxhall Monaro V8. It's awesome."

"OK," I said but noticed mum was ready to fly off the handle again. "Work experience means people will ask you to do things you may not like. That means you can't react like you did at school today because you didn't want to put on your tie."

"It was on!" he responded loudly with indignation. "It was me mate who pulled it over me 'ed." A smirk stretched across his face with the memory. "Fucking bitch!"

"Don't swear!" Mrs Bilson interjected. "Charlie's right, you can't go mad all the time, Gareth. Haven't you noticed folks are gettin' really fed up wi' yer? You can't afford to get excluded one more time otherwise you'll get excluded permanently and I 'ave no idea what I'd do then."

He stood there finding the coving on the ceiling extremely interesting. My eye was drawn up too and I noticed small flecks of plaster on the surface. He must have plastered the wall with his dad in the summer before his dad left home.

"I can't sit 'ere no longer anyway. I need to get off to me appointment. And don't think you're stopping 'ere"—she pointed at Gareth—"I want yer key. You're gonna 'ave to go to your dad's."

"He's not picking me up until four," he replied dismally. "What am I gonna do until then?"

"I don't care. You should be in school," she replied with finality.

"I can take him if you like," I said.

"You can if yer want but I need to go now." Without any further discourse, she stood and ushered both of us to the door.

"Gareth," she pleaded, "can you please stay out of trouble. I can't handle it anymore."

"Yes, mum," he said. At that moment, he just looked like a lost little boy. I was willing her to take him in her arms and just hug him. Instead, she started to close the door on us.

"I'll ring yer later," she said and with that, the door closed.

Gareth jumped into the passenger seat of my car and looked around.

"Is this a three litre?" he asked.

"Yes," I said while I turned off the street and into the main traffic.

"How fast can it go? I bet it can shift," he said.

"When we get inter't countryside, can I 'ave a go?"

I just looked at him with incredulity.

"I can do it yer know," he said trying to reassure me.

"I can drive me dad's car and me mate's Fiesta."

"I bet you can," I replied. "But the fact remains that even if the chances of you crashing this car are as remote as the chance of me winning the lottery, I'm not even going to buy a ticket."

He looked confused. "What d' yer mean?"

"What I mean is that while ever there's a chance of me ruining my reputation, losing my business and possibly putting you in hospital and me in prison, you're not having a go. I'm not even going to stop and let you sit in the passenger seat with the key out."

"Me dad would," he said.

"I'm not your dad," I responded. "I'm here to find out what work experience would suit you." And with that, I drove on, none the wiser as to what work experience would suit because what Gareth really needed above all else was his mum and dad.

Despite my reservations about Gareth, Shelly insisted that I find him a work placement. Therefore, I found a good supportive position at the Car Factory where I felt he could create as little disruption as possible, although I had legitimate reservations about his light fingers. However, the Car Factory has taken a number of students over the years and tends to keep them out of trouble by getting them to assemble bikes in their warehouse and I thought this would fit well with Gareth's interests in machinery.

Next day, I arranged to collect him from his dad's house at around 10 o'clock and I was there around 5 minutes beforehand. However, it was immediately apparent that Gareth wasn't in the right frame of mind to go. When I come across a situation like this, I don't like to jeopardise any employer relationships by placing a student with a bad attitude, so I tend to cancel and come up with an appropriate excuse. In this case, Gareth was standing with his head bowed, hands in pockets, completely disinterested in the world. His dad was bustling about gathering things together as though he was running late. The two people looked so at odds with one another.

"How are you?" I asked politely.

"Alright," he replied.

"Are you ready for your meeting?"

"S'pose so."

"What does that mean?"

"Dunno."

"I'm just looking for a bit of reassurance that you're up for this, that's all," I explained.

Silence.

"Do you want to go to the Car Factory?" I repeated.

"Dunno."

"Come on, Gareth, I need to know that you're happy to do this because these are busy people and they need to know that you are interested in working with them."

Another prolonged silence. All the while dad was bustling about in the background.

"Gareth, I don't want to ask you to do something you don't want to do, so I need you to tell me whether you're interested in doing work experience or not."

I knew what the answer was; he didn't want to go, for no other reason than to spend time with his mum. Living with his dad meant he now had very little contact with her during the week, so he was obviously engineering opportunities to be with her whenever he could, even if she didn't want him there.

He just shrugged his shoulders and therefore I made a decision.

"I'm sorry, Gareth, but you're not ready for this, let's forget it, for now, I'll tell them you're ill or something."

He shrugged again but as soon as I opened the door to leave, dad looked aghast.

"What's going on?" he said.

"He's not ready I'm afraid." My reply sounded lame, so I continued. "He needs to show commitment to going otherwise it will fail. He needs to understand the expectations people have when they take on someone for work experience; he's just not ready."

The disappointment was palpable.

"You're not comin' wi' me!" he barked. "I'm going to do a bit of business. You'll have to go to your mum's."

I don't think Gareth was bothered so long as he had a reason to be with her. I said my goodbyes and gave my feedback to Shelly. Her disappointment was also obvious but at last, she revealed she had been thinking more deeply about the Bilsons. I think she had been hoping to get things fixed without having to get any more involved. Well, now she had to.

"It's pretty obvious," she said. "Gareth needs to spend more time with his mum and she needs to understand that he needs her to mother him. Treat him like her child rather than like something she stood in. It's not his fault his dad ran off with someone else. Leave it with me for a week or so and I'll come back to you."

Sure enough, after a couple of weeks before I heard again from Shelly, who declared that mum now realised she'd not been there for Gareth. She added that things had settled to such an extent that Gareth was now spending Friday and Saturday nights with mum. I, therefore, agreed we would try work experience again.

On my next visit, things were indeed very different. Mum answered the door.

"Hiya love. Come in, he's just getting his shoes on." She stepped into the kitchen and shouted back. "How long d' yer think yer'll be? I've got t'get into town for 11, will you be back be then?"

"No problem," I replied. "We'll be about 10 minutes, no more so we'll be back for half-past 10."

"Brilliant." She turned to Gareth and wiped his face with a cloth. "Good luck, sweetheart. Love you."

"Love you too, mum," he said.

With that, we left to meet the manager, Steve. He was a nice guy and he showed Gareth around the store and into the warehouse.

"With the run-up to Christmas, we spend most of our time building bikes," he said enthusiastically. "So you could really help us with that if you want."

"Great," replied Gareth. "I've got a mountain bike but it's at a mate's house."

This exchange was typical of a student interview; very low-key with the student not really knowing how to handle it. The thing is you can't really prepare them either. Often they're too nervous to remember your advice so you're better off not saying anything at all and hoping they don't say something that's too stupid. Gareth was therefore doing OK.

"So when can he start?" Steve asked.

"Tomorrow?" I asked. "What do you think, Gareth?"

"OK," he said. "What time will I finish?" My heart sank.

"You'll be doing school hours," I said. "9 until 3:30."

"Right," he replied, and that was that. Steve didn't say anything, he was used to it. He once told me that my students could be more reliable than his permanent staff, so his expectations weren't massive.

The next day I took Gareth myself and for the next 2 weeks, all went well until we broke up for Christmas. On the return of the New Year, I went to see him at work but found he was not in the best of moods.

"I don't like it, it's borin'," he said.

"What is?"

"This." He pointed at the bike he was working on. "They make me take all the boxes outside and put them in a skip, even when it's snowin'."

Diddums I thought. "What do you expect, Gareth?" I said. "If you didn't do that, soon the place would be piled high with cardboard. Not only would this prevent you from moving around, it would be a fire hazard."

He looked suspiciously happy at the thought.

"I'm off," he said.

"Where?"

"Home."

"You can't, your mum will be working," I said. I noticed that he was thinking about that fact.

"What did you get for Christmas?" I asked, trying to change the subject only to find I would make the situation infinitely worse.

"Nowt. Me dad spent more on his new girlfriend than he did on me. He told me he would get me summat after he got paid in January." He paced about, throwing imaginary punches like a professional boxer.

"What about from your mum?"

"She gave me £20. That's it." He then did a little shuffle, threw some more punches and set off for the exit.

"You can take me in your car and I can have a go," he said.

"No chance. You need to stay here and finish that bike," I replied. With that, he strode back to the bench, put down the tool he was holding and headed out of the back of the warehouse through a small door. I followed him and watched incredulously as he crossed the car park and down a footpath between hedgerows.

Just then, Steve entered the warehouse and saw me at the door. "What's up?" he asked.

"It's Gareth, he's walked off down that footpath," I said, pointing across the car park to a rapidly shrinking figure heading away from us.

"Oh, don't worry about that. It's a dead end. He'll be back in about 5 minutes."

Sure enough, 5 minutes later, he was back but he didn't stop. He carried on across the car park, across the front of the store and into the trading estate. We just looked at each other.

"Stupid little bugger," said Steve. "It's 3 miles to town that way." It was starting to snow.

I looked at the heavens. "I'll call his mum."

She answered immediately. I explained the situation I was in. Her reply was emphatic, "He's not comin' 'ere, I've got someone in, I'm doing their nails," she said.

"He's walked off though and it's started to snow. What do you want me to do?" I replied.

"Take him back t'work, I'm busy." And with that, she cut me off.

Without much choice, I jumped in my car and set off after Gareth. I hadn't gone far when I saw him walking slowly along the side of the road. I pulled up and noticed he was on the phone. I waited until he'd finished, which didn't take long.

"Get in," I said. He ignored me and turned around the way he had come, meaning I had to drive a bit further to find a junction to turn around, so I could do the same. The snow was getting heavier now, coming down in large lumps, catching immediately on the ground and forming a layer of icing sugar on every surface. I caught up with Gareth again.

"Gareth!" I shouted. "Get in, it's snowing." He still ignored me. "Gareth!" I shouted again. "I could do without this messing around. I don't care for people who ignore me."

"That's typical of people like you," he retorted. "yer don't care, so you can fuck off."

I rang his mum again. "I'm sorry," I said, "but he won't get in the car and now he's being abusive."

"I know," she replied. "I've just spoken to him."

"Mrs Bilson, if Gareth doesn't get in the car and you won't have him, what am I supposed to do?" I pleaded.

"Put him on the phone," she said, so I called Gareth who eventually stopped walking. His hair had a layer of snow on top and his eyelashes were struggling to cope with the blizzard conditions, making him blink constantly.

"Your mum wants a word," I said and with that, I passed him the phone. What ensued was a long, expletive-laden conversation but in the end, he passed me back the phone.

Mrs Bilson just said 3 words: "Bring 'im 'ome." So I did.

We never said another word to each other during the journey and when I dropped him off, he didn't say goodbye or thank you, he simply knocked on the door and waited until his mum let him in without saying anything herself. She did not acknowledge him or me; she just slowly closed the door.

It was of no surprise to me that after ignoring the warnings, the interventions and help offered to the family that the school head finally pulled the trigger on Gareth's school career and he was permanently excluded.

Sadly, that was the last I ever saw of Gareth Bilson.

I Need a Hero

Beth stretched like a cat about to climb out of its basket. Again, I realised how small she was. Boyish hips, small feet and long hair of varying colours. Her eyebrows looked like brooding slugs, although the eyes beneath still shone like the first time I met her, except this time she had an air of absolute confidence about her. The hair dressing salon had been fantastic for her well-being. Both Tina and Tracey had worked hard to bring Beth into the land of the living. They started by asking her to take customer coats and bags. She then took on the task of making coffees and teas and now she was washing ladies' hair. They had done this on numerous occasions for numerous other girls, helping them build their confidence in a safe environment.

One of my previous students, Harriet, had spent a turbulent year at the salon. Turbulent because she'd moved out of her home to live with her nan who was subsequently diagnosed with cancer, prompting a swift return home during which her father died. Mum had gone off the rails so Harriet had then to go and live with her sister. School was also extremely worried about Harriet as she had a circle of much older friends and it looked to all the world like she was being groomed by shady, older men. Yet things turned out better than everyone had hoped. On the verge of being dumped in a hostel after falling out with her sister, Harriet found a flat with a girlfriend and she used this stability to keep her studies up and attend work experience. On the back of this resolute attitude, she had gone to college and was now working at the salon part-time. Harriet's year of crisis had a happy ending, mainly because Tracey and Tina had shown such belief in her and had given her as much encouragement as they could to keep her engaged.

The salon had started when both Tina and Tracey had fallen out with their old boss and decided to set up on their own, taking the vast majority of the customers with them in the process. I think they realised they needed to move on when they made the 'Old battle axe' a cup of tea with a tea bag that had dropped into the toilet bowl. Sense overcame them as, just as the old dear was about to take a sip, Tracey nudged her arm sending a cascade of hot, contaminated tea all over her apron and feet, prompting an immediate sacking. This was the ideal outcome and gave them both the opportunity to move on without guilt.

Both girls were chirpy, happy souls, filled with advice about life, love, men and work but not necessarily in that order! Men were the main topic of the day with scores of elderly ladies reliving their past, present and futures, discussing the latest hottie and nudging the conversation along with innuendo. My visits were often punctuated with humour and ogling eyes. I'm not the best eye candy in the world but a trip to the salon often left me feeling 10 feet tall. We are, after all, vain beings who love a compliment, particularly when we get older. I would also give as good as I got, so the visits would fly by.

Those visits to see Beth and the girls were often punctuated with revealing anecdotes and personal details. Conscious that I did not want to be seen as robotic as some social workers can be, I would often reveal a few snippets about my personal life to help students trust me and identify with me. I felt safe doing that at the salon as they were such fantastic people.

Beth stretched again.

"Why are you so tired?" I asked.

"I hardly got any sleep," she replied.

"Why?"

"Well, you know mum threatened to take my phone off me when I didn't want to start here? Well, we had a massive argument and she said I couldn't have Louie around if I was going to be like that."

"Who's Louie?" I asked.

"He's my boyfriend. So I didn't see him for like ages but I got a bit fed up of being on my own so I sent him a message to come around when my mum went out to book club last night," she replied.

"Okayyyy," I said wondering what was coming next.

"So he comes around and we're in my room," she said. I must have raised my eyebrows because she quickly continued. "Nothing like that! We were watching Netflix. Anyway, I heard the front door go and my mum calls out, 'Bethany darling, I'm back, book club is cancelled'. So then I'm really scared, so I get Louie to climb in the wardrobe and it's rattling and banging but he gets in just in time. Good job, as well as my mum opens the door to my room, asking me if I'm OK!" She stopped for a breath.

"What were you doing, love?" she asks me.

"Putting my clothes away," I said. "I dropped a coat hanger in the wardrobe." She just raised an eye and said, "It's hot in here, why don't you open a window."

I'm like, "mum, no I'm fine and eventually, she leaves." She stops and grins.

"So what happened next?" I asked, fascinated.

"Well, my mum's room is next to mine, so I waited until she started snoring because she snores like mad. I can hardly sleep sometimes it's that bad. Anyway, it took like forever. Louie's in the wardrobe whispering that he's in agony and I'm like shut up! So at about 2 am, mum's proper going for it so I sneak Louie out of the wardrobe, out of my room and out of the house. I was more scared then than ever!"

"Did your mum wake up?" I was still fascinated.

"No, thank God but she gave me a funny look this morning. I don't know why she doesn't like Louie."

"How old is he?" I asked out of curiosity.

"19," she replied. "It's fine though, I think he's on the autism spectrum which is why he's so immature."

"Might be why she's a bit prickly, Beth," I responded knowing full well why mum wasn't sure about him. "I'm not sure I would be happy with my daughter hanging around with someone 4 years older than her."

She looked a little despondent with that so I cheered her up as best I could with my own anecdote.

"Your story reminds me of when I was a teenager," I said. She looked back at me tilting her head slightly in curiosity. Beth's story had also attracted the girls' attention too, so I now had a bigger audience.

"I had a girlfriend whose mum and dad were Methodists. I used to go around and listen to records on her record player," I began.

"I bet you did." Tracey winked. I ignored her but smiled and continued.

"We were only 15 so being in her bedroom was a big no, no but it was the summer holidays and there had been a group of us in the house listening to music. However, most people had gone home for tea and I was about to leave when her dad came home from work a little bit early. My girlfriend just froze and then started shoving me under the bed, I had no idea what was going on. I was there for 2 hours. This was all before mobile phones so when I got home, my mother hit the roof wondering where I was. I didn't have the heart to tell her the truth so I lied and said I'd gone to town to meet some friends and spent my bus money on fast food and had to walk home. She said I deserved the fact that I'd had no tea."

"Told you he was a wrong 'un," said Tracey and went back to work.

Beth cheered up and told me a bit more about Louie and about the fact he didn't have a job, or any qualifications but also how her own mum couldn't talk having had 2 failed marriages to 2 idiots. I suppose Beth failed to spot that history may be repeating itself. That is certainly a characteristic of my job, how families seem to pass on their bad habits as much as their good ones.

Beth wasn't the most enthusiastic student I had ever worked with but she was humorous, honest and therefore, likeable. On my next visit, we had a further tale of woe. While washing a lady's hair, Beth had inadvertently spilt water down the back of Mrs Millington, wetting her through down to her underwear. Beth had ignored what had happened and carried on and poor Mrs Millington being so embarrassed just shed a little tear as Tina dried her off and gave her a strong cup of tea. Beth didn't see the point in apologising either because she was embarrassed or more likely because she didn't have a clue about empathy. As I pointed out to her, Mrs Millington probably has her hair done more times than she needs because she enjoys the company and chatter. For that reason, Mrs Millington deserved to be treated better. She'd probably spent a lifetime looking after others but they'd all grown up and moved away and she probably had friends and close loved ones that had died and passed on. She was therefore very likely to be lonely, spending most of her time watching puerile day time TV, with endless repeats and with adverts advising that she improve her life insurance policy in order to get a free pen. Beth looked distraught at the thought and apologised to the girls and Mrs Millington, the next time she came in. Like most teenagers, she lived in a world where self-obsession is glorified, so she never gave Mrs Millington a second thought. Mrs Millington was lonely and that is one of the hardest things to appreciate for a young person. However, Beth was getting the message and was growing up quickly, all thanks to her experience in the salon.

My time with Beth was coming to a close and the school were increasingly concerned about the choices she would make on her step towards adulthood. Beth being Beth, she was more concerned about her love life and phone contract than her future so she spent most of her time dithering over whether an apprenticeship or college would be the best option. We saw a slight increase in her anxiety levels as she re-lived her experience of college which had made her run out of the classroom earlier in the year. College wasn't for her but she didn't want to do an apprenticeship yet. Without the girls, we may never have moved Beth into a decision to go to college; it was the best option because although she played the part of the dopey imp from time to time, she was intelligent and needed just a year or two more to allow her intelligence a chance to flourish. I can't thank Tina and Tracey enough for that.

However, for every Tracey and Tina, there are dozens of those that flatly refuse to help, or even worse, dangle the carrot that they would like to help but just need to check with head office. The ones who flatly refuse tend to fall into 2 categories. Firstly, there are those that have had students before, often to help out a friend or family member. The biggest gripe coming from this group is that the students do a lot of standing around looking at their phones.

Ibra and I have discussed this many times and our advice to prospective employers is to have good policies in place to set student expectations and also be prepared to have time and patience in at least getting the student started. Unfortunately, patience is in short supply and employers from this group tend to be abusive or downright rude when we ask them if they'll try again. They forget that someone made an effort with them when they were first starting out.

This is also true with the second group and I have to say it tends to be the bigger companies with well-scripted statements on inclusivity and corporate social responsibility that are the biggest culprits.

Inclusivity is the desire to ensure all members of society are given equal opportunities in their businesses. Clearly, this doesn't extend to students looking for work experience.

Supermarkets, building firms, DIY chains, fast food outlets, electrical contractors, etc, etc simply give me an email address for HR and then, nothing. Not one manager has the authority to make a decision on behalf of their store so we get pushed upstairs to a nameless bunch of people who would rather side-step the opportunity than offer to help younger people onto the career ladder.

I get ignored a lot.

Corporate social responsibility is similar in that it's a grand statement that basically says a company recognises its social impact and is accountable for it. So an example would be that a supermarket may sell high sugar content fizzy drinks to kids and offset the guilt by sponsoring a football tournament. I believe there are moves to change this situation as with caffeine drinks but the drive to change doesn't come from the industry itself. And no amount of football tournament sponsorship can offset the harm caused to those kids who don't play football. That's the vast majority of kids, by the way.

I just wish bigger businesses would stop treating us like idiots and engage with the community in a heartfelt way. Maybe it would prevent people like me from being so cynical about their motives. Just give the kids a chance.

It is the final group however that causes us such a big headache on a daily basis. We don't bother with the big companies any more but there are those that used to be small companies but wish to be big, that do have managers that can make decisions for themselves.

They'll often say yes but ask us to call them back in a few days when they've considered the situation. So, we'll call back but more often than not they don't answer, therefore we'll then send a text to their mobile and in all likelihood, get no reply. The next option is to email them, though emails tend to disappear into the internet never to be seen again. As a last resort, we go back and visit the business again but we'll usually be greeted by a look akin to 'Oh no, not him again' and be asked to come back tomorrow as it's such a busy time. Out of desperation, we go back the day after and at last they'll give us an honest answer.

No, we're just too busy.

Why didn't you say that in the first place?

There's definitely an element in society that don't know what answer to give; the type of people who sit on the fence and go with the majority depending on where the wind is blowing from. They think they should help because that would be the right thing to do. But they don't actually want to help but equally don't want to be seen as the bad guys. People in these roles, the middle managers, only want to do something that will enhance their status rather than do the right thing, so they hedge their bets trying to put me and Ibra off without saying no, hoping we will go away. But we don't. Infuriating though it may be, we want to hear the words come from their own lips.

I have this dream every so often where one of the senior managers in these companies, or in the corporates, thinks work experience is an amazing idea for 14–16-year-olds and then all these middle managers would be fighting like cat and dog to be my friend. Fat chance.

Thus, we rely on the small people in this world, the ones with the most to lose but the ones with the most to give, like Tina and Tracey. Hairdressers, builders, carpenters, electricians, shopkeepers and mechanics, all offering opportunities to young people, prepared to give them a chance. These kids may be flaky, unreliable and arrogant but we can laugh at their posturing, ignore the lateness and tiredness, the yawning and the feckless fumbling and the standing around looking gormless because in the end, they can be changed. At the end of Year 11, when they've turned 16, they change to such a degree that they're often offered employment, which is so far removed from the situation they would have been in if they hadn't done work experience.

These good employers make us feel like a miracle workers. "The horse whisperers of work experience", as one teacher once described what we do. However, it is the employers who do the hard yards. We get the students through the door, over the threshold, bleary-eyed and nervous, we give them the nudge to get them started, and show patience when they're feigning illness or struggling to get out of bed. But it's the employers who straighten them out, become their role models and teach them the tricks of the trade that give them confidence. They are the real heroes.

Ain't No Mountain High Enough

Dominic Tordoff drew on a cigarette and then sipped at his tea. He looked up at me with a sneer.

"Why are you 'ere?" he said flashing the scaffolding in his mouth.

"To see you, make sure that you're doing alright and turning up to your placement," I said.

"Well, 'ere I am, havin' a tea break," he replied. He hadn't changed and still had no respect for me whatsoever.

"I've got some news for you actually," I said wishing I really didn't have. "Ms Salbanio has organised a day out at an outward-bound event and she was wondering if you would like to go."

When Ms Salbanio had rung me she had asked my opinion on how Dominic would take the offer of a day out. I was honest and said I thought he'd take it but didn't think it would do anything for him. However, she was insistent that I take him and that we take our time.

Dominic was quick to respond. "Owt to get me out er school," he replied. He tentatively puffed on his cigarette. It was more for show than enjoyment. "When is it?" he asked.

"A week on Thursday. We're going over to the Western Dales to climb Ingleborough," I said.

"Ingleborough?" he asked. "What's that?"

"It's one of Yorkshire's 3 peaks," I responded. "It's about 2000 feet high and should take 3–4 hours to complete. If we set off at around 10 am, we should be back in town for about half 3."

"Are you comin' as well?" he said, clearly unimpressed at the prospect of my company.

"Yes, I was pleased to be asked because I like being outdoors," I said. He didn't reply and simply turned to finish his tea.

"Back to work," he eventually declared, straining to stand up and with that, he walked off. I followed him into the building and said hello to Christopher the manager. When Dominic had gone into the warehouse, I asked Christopher if everything was OK.

"Fine," he said. "He sort of comes and goes as he pleases. I feel it's best to let him do that as I don't want to trigger any other depressive episode." I must have rolled my eyes involuntarily.

He looked at me quizzically as I replied, "Dominic is..."—I paused—"...difficult to get a grip of." I was struggling to be diplomatic. "What I mean is that he is very controlling. I just don't want him to be taking advantage."

"It suits us at the moment," said Christopher.

"In that case," I replied, "we can just keep an eye on things."

A week later, I pulled into the Yorkshire Dales National car park in Ingleton at approximately 10 am in the morning. It was a fine day and as things were going, it was likely to be a very good summer. The ride over to Ingleton had been uneventful, Dominic had snoozed most of the way and didn't make any effort to break up the journey for my benefit. Once out of the car, we gathered our things and met with a local ranger called Matt who had been assigned as the guide for our walk. Matt was a well-meaning young man, very much in his element, slightly balding, fair-haired and rosy-cheeked from spending most of his time outdoors. Matt had selected the route for our walk and suggested we would be back at around 2:30 pm and once he had gone through the health and safety information, we set off.

Being a warm day, the heat rose from the pathways in pleasant waves, the grass waving in the slight breeze and the sheep and lambs lazily grazing in the fields. The fells climbed in front of us in great rolling mounds, punctured with outcrops of stone and copses of trees. It looked daunting but Dominic actually looked worried.

"Are you OK?" I asked.

"Fine," he responded. "When will we get back?"

"About 2:30 pm," said Matt.

Dominic turned to me. "So when will we get back to town?" he asked.

"Well, it took roughly an hour to get here, so around 3:30 pm?" I said shrugging my shoulders. "Why, what's so important that we need to get back?" I asked. I was conscious that Ms Salbanio had suggested we took our time but I sensed Dominic didn't want to hang around.

"I've got an appointment at 4 o'clock," he said. *What appointment? I thought. The orthodontist again?* However, I considered it best not to challenge him about that, for all I knew, he could have booked salsa dancing lessons.

I simply replied, "Well, in that case, we should be fine."

As we climbed, we assumed a pattern to our progress where Matt went ahead pointing out the features of the landscape almost to himself. I was slightly behind straining my interested ears and behind me around 20 yards further back was Dominic, shuffling along in his long-folded gait, hoodie tied around his waist, t-shirt flapping in the breeze which grew stronger as we climbed. He kept looking at his phone, constantly checking the time and messages.

"You're wasting your time," shouted Matt. "There's no signal up here." And with that, Dominic put his phone back in his pocket.

As we continued our progress, we eventually came to the mouth of Gaping Gyll, the deepest cave in England. It was fairly unimpressive to look at from above but was the height of York Cathedral underground. Dominic was unimpressed no matter how much effort Matt made to engage him on the wonders of Yorkshire's underground world.

And so we continued. Before long, we were scrambling to the lower slopes of Little Ingleborough, a scree-laden outcrop glued to the side of our main destination – Ingleborough itself. In time, we had scrambled to the top and could look over to the east and the flattened top of the mountain. Having strode east for a quarter of a mile, we were soon scrambling up to the top and before long, we were sitting in the cross-shaped shelter of the summit eating our sandwiches. The surface was a broad, exposed circle of stone and thin grass. At one time, the top of Ingleborough had been an ancient fort. Although the weather was fair, it was clear in my mind that only an ancient idiot would live up there, particularly in winter. Unfortunately, all the history, geology and demography of the landscape around us fell on deaf ears. Dominic was only interested in one thing; the time.

"How long are we gonna' sit here?" he said with a bluntness only reserved for the truly conscious-less.

"We'll have a few minutes walking around the top and then we'll set off back," replied Matt, looking a little perturbed by Dominic's curt words.

Dominic didn't respond; he just looked at his phone. It was devoid of any update as we were off-grid, so he pretended it was full of new information and proceeded to look through it with an avid interest only experienced by those who have been stood up on a blind date and are sitting on their own in a restaurant full of couples in love.

He jumped up and started pacing around trying to force an early return down the mountain. I watched him for a moment and then tried some reassurance.

"It's only 12:30 and it'll be quicker going back, so we've plenty of time," I said.

He ignored me as he had Matt and went off further to the east where the path falls in a long stretch towards Horton in Ribblesdale.

Matt and I decided on the same tactic and ignored him. However, he had set off with purpose and stepped off the hill-top and down the steep grassy bank on the eastern side of the hill. Having seen him disappear, I panicked and ran after him. As I reached the edge of the hill, he had reached the stony track below.

"Dominic!" I had to shout to get his attention. "Dominic! Where are you going? You can't go that way, it's 6 miles to Horton and 6 miles in completely the opposite direction to where the car is!"

"I'll get the bus!" he shouted back.

"What bus?" I replied. "There are no buses running around here!"

"A taxi then!" he shouted back petulantly. By this time, Matt had reached my side.

"There are no taxis either, Dominic, we're in the middle of nowhere!" I shouted with exasperation.

Matt, sensing my frustration, also shouted, "He's right, Dominic, you'll get back a lot later going that way, it's best to go back the way we came!"

Dominic hesitated. Clearly, he was torn between following someone else's advice over his own decision. If Matt hadn't intervened, I'm sure Dominic would have dragged us all off towards Horton. He turned and came back towards us. As he reached the top, he strode straight past us and as we hesitated, expecting to have a word with him, he called out, "Come on then, let's get back" and continued walking.Both Matt and I looked at each other and shrugged our shoulders with Matt mouthing the words, "What's up with him?"

"I've no idea," I whispered back and we set off back to the shelter where we collected our things and set off back the way we had come.

As with any jaunt on a warm day at a place like the slopes of Ingleborough, there are lots of other people around. We'd spent most of our journey saying hello to other ramblers and passing the time of day but as we descended from Little Ingleborough, a lady approached us ashen-faced and breathless having had to run to catch us up.

"Help me!" she said with urgency. "Can you help me?"

"What's wrong?" asked Matt, suddenly becoming more alert.

"It's my husband; he's just taken a tumble and twisted his ankle. I think it's broken as he's refusing to move," she said.

"Where is he?" asked Matt, removing his backpack.

"Back up the track as you start to drop down over the boulders," she explained. "Just there." She was pointing to a prone figure massaging his leg approximately 200 yards away.

"OK," said Matt, "don't worry, I'm a Park Ranger, I'll radio into the base and explain the situation. There's a good chance that if your husband's injury is bad enough, he might need to be extracted by mountain rescue or even helicopter, looking at the terrain." He was scanning the position of the casualty with an expert eye.

While all this was going on, Dominic continued his progress. I called for him to stop and he reluctantly halted 50 yards ahead. Both Matt and I then ran back towards the casualty as Matt made a radio call to the base to let them know there was a potential shout. Dominic started shuffling back in our direction and eventually stood over us as Matt examined the man's leg. The ankle was swollen and angry and the man was clearly in pain.

"How long's this gonna' take?" wailed Dominic. Matt ignored him and spoke to the casualty and his wife.

"This ankle looks like it's in a bad way, have you tried standing on it?" The man shook his head and showed no sign of wanting to try.

"Right, it seems we need some help." He then called base again and ordered medical help and in due course mountain rescue.

"Right, so everything's organised, we just have to wait for the team to arrive," he said.

In the meantime, we introduced ourselves and they explained they were Brian and Dorothy Porter from Norfolk who were on a walking holiday. All the while Dominic was pacing around in irritation but his curiosity was stopping him from moving off without seeing what happened next.

After approximately 20 minutes, we could hear the rotor of a distant helicopter and soon we could see the outline of a bright yellow air ambulance on the route from its base near Thirsk. We all watched it circle the area and eventually, settle on a patch of land 300 yards away. Matt went to speak with the paramedics and guided them to where Brian was sitting among the rocks. Now the medical team had arrived, you could sense both Brian and Dorothy were relieved. After another 10 minutes or so a 110, 8-seater Land rover appeared over a small hillock behind the helicopter and parked 50 yards or so beyond it. Before long a team of 6 or 7 people were also with Brian, armed with a stretcher and roped equipment for extracting him from among the rocks and down the slope to where the helicopter sat.

After a full assessment of the casualty and the administration of pain killers, he had a splint fitted to his lower leg and was manoeuvred onto the stretcher. After another 20 minutes or so, the mountain rescue team had slowly moved him by carrying and sliding his stretcher down the slope and were now moving slowly but with purpose towards the helicopter.

We all followed the group and watched as they put Brian in the back of the helicopter. By now, there was a healthy crowd curious to see what had happened with their phones at the ready to photograph the helicopter as it took off. The pilot explained to Dorothy and her husband that they would fly him to the Leeds General Infirmary and that Dorothy could make her way there to meet him once the mountain rescue team had given her a lift back to Ingleton where she could pick up her car from the hotel they were staying in.

Sure enough, the helicopter was soon in the air, it carried out a swooping circle of the area and then disappeared with purpose to the south.

Matt and I walked with Dorothy to the mountain rescue team Land rover and wished her luck in meeting up with her husband. He would only need 15 minutes to get to Leeds but it would take her at least an hour and a half to make the same journey. It was at that moment that we noticed Dominic wasn't there. I looked around and although there were many faces still milling around. His wasn't one of them.

"Has anyone seen a young lad about 16, 6 ft tall, thin, with braces on his teeth?" I asked with desperation.

"Yes," said one of the mountain rescue team. "About 10 minutes ago, he asked for a lift to Ingleton but I refused as we needed all the seats to get the team out. He set off towards Ingleton straight away."

"Oh for God's sake," I said out loud. "That lad is the bane of my life!"

Matt and I set off at a run in an attempt to catch him but no matter how hard we pushed, we couldn't get near him and I had no idea where he was. It was around 3:30 pm when we got back to the car and Dominic was nowhere to be seen, all I could hope for now was that I could get him on the phone. As I dialled the number, I was beyond fear for the lad, instead I was extremely angry.

He answered straight away.

"Where are you?" I barked.

"On the main road, tryin' to get a lift," he replied with a hint of panic in his voice.

"Don't move!" I shouted and said my goodbyes to Matt, I went to get him.

Sure enough, there he was trying desperately to flag down a passing car. It was obvious that no one was going to offer him a lift; he had a look of sheer panic on his face.

"Get in!" I shouted. "And don't you ever do that to me again. What the hell is going on?"

"I just needed to get back before 4 o'clock," he said.

"Fine but when there's been an accident, we have to change our plans and help as much as we can," I said. "So what's the big deal about this appointment and don't give me any more bullshit about orthodontists, counsellors and the like, just give me the bloody truth." I was incandescent with anger and for the first time in our relationship, Dominic was taking notice of me.

"I can't say," he muttered. "They'll kill me."

"Who will?" I asked.

"I'm gonna 'ave to ring 'em to say I'm late," he said absent-mindedly and dialled into his phone. The conversation was very one way; I could just make out a very angry voice pointing out that if this happened again, there would be drastic consequences. Dominic's face went pale and then white as a sheet. He dropped his face into his hands and rubbed his eyes until they were red.

"Dominic, what the hell is going on?" I repeated.

"Please don't ask, sir," he pleaded. "I can't tell yer"

"I can't force you to tell me," I replied, "but I can assure you it is pretty obvious you are in serious trouble and the longer you leave it, the worse your problems are going to get," I said with finality.

He looked scared, deathly scared and at that point I realised Dominic was on the verge of tears.

"How much does your mum know about this?" I asked.

"Nowt, so please don't tell her." He was pleading again.

"I'm sorry, Dominic, but it's not my job to ignore a situation that has got you so badly spooked. I'm going to have to speak to everyone that needs to know, your mum, school, even the police."

He looked out of the window and took a deep breath.

"Look, Dom," I continued, trying to get closer to him. "Maybe I can help?" I paused before I dropped the question that had been niggling at the back of my mind. Only now was I able to grasp it.

"Is it drugs?"

There was a long silence, all we could hear was the rumble of the car tyres on the road and the swoosh at every passing car and lorry. He didn't deny it, so I drew my own conclusions and the more we travelled in silence, the more the pieces of this complicated jigsaw began to fall into place.

Once we were back, I dropped him off in town and he bolted from the car at a rate of knots. I had by now pieced the jigsaw together, and I just needed confirmation from Ms Salbanio regarding my conclusions. Having contacted the school, Ms Salbanio agreed with what I thought as she had her own suspicions, hence why she advised that we took our time out on the walk up Ingleborough. She apologised for putting me in that situation but as I explained, the rambler breaking his ankle created an inevitable delay anyway. Ms Salbanio then contacted both his mum and the police and within a few days, mum and Dominic were in Spain on an extended holiday while the police attempted to round-up the culprits that had put Dominic in such a vulnerable situation.

So what had happened?

It all began with Dillon, Dominic's long standing friend. Dillon was dealing drugs via the 'County Lines'.

County lines are the methods with which inner-city drug gangs communicate with local dealers who work on their behalf. They use burner phones that are unregistered to communicate with their dealers and use vulnerable local kids to distribute the drugs to their local network. This way they remain anonymous but keep control of the local trade. The young kids are also easy to scare and are easily replaced if things go wrong.

When Benjy, Dillon's dad discovered what was going on, he immediately acted by taking Dillon to Ireland, leaving Dillon's network free of a local dealer. As Dominic was in Dillon's thrall, he jumped at the chance of taking over the trade.

Things were going well for Dominic; he was making good money and was managing to keep myself and the school off his back by doing the minimum level of work experience without attracting too much suspicion. However, he hadn't banked on Ms Salbanio knowing about Dillon. Therefore, she always had her suspicions that he was up to no good. The trip to Ingleborough was her attempt to get him out of the area and therefore, flush the truth out of him and it had worked, although in an unexpected manner.

That day was the day that Dominic was to collect his stash of drugs for the week. He was to meet someone he didn't know in the centre of town at 4 o'clock and from there, he would be driven out of town where the exchange of money from last week's sales would be made for a new batch of narcotics. The timing of the meeting was critical as there were other young dealers to be met to make the same exchange. As Dominic was running late, the whole operation was under threat and he was panicking that he would get into serious trouble as the cause of the delays. He had heard what could happen to dealers who didn't follow the rules. That was all now immaterial, as he had been swiftly removed from trouble.

The next time I was with Ms Salbanio, she was rather pleased with herself and the fact that her plan had worked out so well. She explained that Dominic had gained a place at college when he returned from Spain, so in September, he would be off the school roll. I expected her to be more relieved, so I asked why she wasn't ecstatic that he was out of her hair.

"Quite simple," she replied. "As we've learned these last few weeks, for every Dillon, there's a Dominic."

"Right," I responded laughing. "But surely, this has been an extreme case? There can't be many families like the Tordoffs."

"That's true," she acknowledged. "But like I said, for every Dillon, there's a Dominic and for every Dominic, there's a Freddie."

"Who's Freddie?" I asked with curiosity.

"Dominic's younger brother," she said. "And he's twice as bad. Worships the ground his brother walks on."

"Sounds ominous," I said.

"It is," she continued. "He's already got a string of exclusions to his name for various misdemeanours. Fighting, stealing, and being downright disruptive and aggressive. He thinks he's a proper little gangster."

"Like Dominic?" I said.

"Yup, just like him but worse," she replied.

"I don't fancy having to deal with him," I declared, making a mental note not to bring his name up again.

"I was worried you might say that," said Ms Salbanio, "because I'd like you to meet him in the next school year to do work experience."

Dreaming of Me

"Yer see that tree there? I did that!" exclaimed Tommy Capstick. "It was in a garden so I took it and shoved it on t' pole."

I was driving him to work experience and could only glance in the general direction of his finger. I could just see a Christmas tree stuck on top of the pole of a road sign 12 feet in the air.

"Some fella saw us doin' it and told me to get down, I just told him to fuck off."

He was just getting into his stride but I was reluctant to listen as his tales tended to be made-up and sprinkled liberally with profanities.

"Said to him I'd smash his teeth in if he didn't jog on," he continued.

I relented, "What did he say?"

"Ha! Nowt," he replied. "Probably shit 'imself."

Tommy's stories had become part and parcel of my week and usually involve stupid pranks, random violence and regular dealings with the police. The thing is Tommy never had evidence of his tom foolery. He never had a scratch or mark on him and he never got arrested, even though he could describe his antics in fine detail and with glowing pride. The thing is I didn't believe half of what he said.

For example, I'd noticed the Christmas tree had been there a couple of months previously and I was sure that I'd seen a man with a ladder putting it there with a sign advertising Christmas tree sales. He'd probably forgotten to take it down. Regardless of the facts, I let Tommy fill the air with his tales.

It was now mid-March and having endured a harsh winter, the tree now looked very sorry for itself. In contrast, the daffodils were in full bloom and the sheep had their very young lambs at their feet, bleating and demanding milk. One of them caught Tommy's eye.

"Lambs!" he said. "Me and Robbie pinched one 'o them last year."

Here we go again, I thought.

"Took it 'ome and kept it in t' shed," he continued.

I didn't bother to ask how he fed it, as I imagine he wasn't the type to keep ewe's milk just in case he felt the urge to steal a lamb. Instead, I prompted him to go on.

"What did you do with it?"

"Went to see t' farmer. Said we found it roamin' around t'village."

"What did he say?" I asked.

"Said it was a crackin' looking lamb and give us £50 for it," he replied in triumph.

"Wow," I said with as much false enthusiasm as I could muster, knowing full well the lambs would have been tagged and sprayed with the farmer's markings so he could have easily identified it. He would more likely give Tommy and his pal an earful for stealing it, rather than £50 for bringing it back.

"Think I might do it again this year," he declared, drawing that particular tale to its conclusion.

We then had a prolonged silence while Tommy put his earphones on to listen to music on his phone, nodding his head and mouthing the obscenities that littered that particular track.

"Fuckin' avin' it," he said as we passed someone walking on the pavement.

"Have what?" I asked.

"Him. The fuckin' tool. Tried to jump me wi' 'is mates."

"Oh, yeah?" I said distantly as I manoeuvred the car into a side street as we were entering the town.

"There were 8 of 'em," he said. "I thought to myself. Fuck that! So I ran off. I'll fuckin' have 'im when he's on his own."

I pulled up at the side of the road.

"Looks like this is the place," I said. Tommy began to gather his things including some amber leaf tobacco, a can of high-energy drink and a sharing packet of Haribos. His lunch was somewhat makeshift, to say the least.

"Aye," he replied, "that's Bob's van."

He climbed out of the car and as I pulled away, we said our goodbyes.

Bob Timble was a landscape gardener who worked on a variety of jobs throughout the district. He had a few lads working for him and therefore, he could take on some of the more challenging commissions. This meant Tommy could learn a variety of things from making mortar, laying stone flags, dry stone walling and building decking, to name a few. However, no matter how hard I tried, Tommy didn't want to talk about his work, he always wanted to tell tales of his adventures, which by now I was convinced were completely made up.

Each day I collected him was no different. I would always ask him how he was, out of politeness. In return, all I heard was how Tommy's asthma was causing him chest pains, how the car crash he had been in was making his arm hurt and how after falling off his bike, his ribs ached so he couldn't sleep. These tales of woe would take approximately 10 minutes or so, after which Tommy would roll a cigarette ready to smoke once he'd left the car. He would then listen to some music and at some random point in the track would make an unexpected outburst.

"Had to laugh this mornin'," he said out of the blue.

"Me two sisters were fightin' like cat and dog. I was pissin' myself laughin'!"

"Oh yeah?" I replied. It had become my standard reply for Tommy.

"They were proper goin' for it. Knockin' all kinds er shit out er one another."

"Oh yeah?"

"Aye. When they'd calmed down a bit, I asked what was up? Chelsea, me eldest sister said that Sheera, me younger sister had stuck a cactus in her 'ead and a load er needles were stuck in it. I'm telling you I was cryin' wi' laughter."

"Where did they get the cactus from?"

"Me mam got 3 of 'em from the supermarket for the living room. I'm tellin' you this cactus was still stuck in 'er 'ead! I had to pull it out but it left some needles behind. She looked like a 'edgehog." He carried on giggling.

Soon enough, we arrived at our destination and gathering his things, Tommy got out of the car. He had been on work experience for 3 weeks by that point and Bob was pleased with his contribution. I had started to feel comfortable that he was settling in and that I may not have to visit him as regularly as I was doing. In the early days, it can pay dividends if we transport students to and from work, as it gets them into a good routine quite quickly but it was potentially time to let Tommy look after himself.

Having dropped him off, I went home to pick up Lauren. She had her eye on a new home and there was a new housing estate being built on the edge of town. Therefore, she had arranged a viewing of the show home and one particular property that was still under construction.

We arrived to be met by a very polished young lady who proceeded to show us around the house. To my surprise, all the rooms were beautifully furnished, including the bedrooms which had all the beds made up and curtains in the windows. The house looked superb. Having then seen our potential new home, I was happy that this could be the one for us and therefore, Lauren and I put our names down for No 26, Badger Corner.

Over the next few weeks, we organised a mortgage and waited impatiently for our new home to be completed. In the meantime, Tommy Capstick was managing to get himself to work or to the place Bob had agreed to collect him, so things were progressing nicely on that front too. I visited him a couple of times, the first of which was to a very large property in Manerton which was having a new stepped garden installed, with raised borders and new decking.

"Where's Tommy?" I asked Bob.

"Inside. He's gone to the toilet."

"Is that wise?" I asked, full in the knowledge that Tommy was very vocal about his ability as a house breaker, not that I believed him but I could envisage him rummaging through the owners prized possessions, taking what he fancied.

"It'll be fine," replied Bob. "I made him take his boots off."

With that, Tommy emerged onto the patio through some double doors and sure enough, he was in stockinged feet. I stared at his pockets looking for the tell-tale sign of a bulge where he might have stashed the loot but there was nothing to show.

It will be fine, I thought. Tommy makes most of this stuff up anyway.

The next time I visited him was to another large property a few miles away from Manerton at Great Siveton. The renovation work was extensive, including a new patio, a large dry stone walled area for better shelter and a stone-built barbeque. When I arrived, Tommy was just entering the house, pausing to remove his boots.

"Where's he going?" I asked Bob.

"Toilet," he replied. "I swear the lad's got the bladder of a mouse. He's forever going to the loo."

After 5 minutes, Tommy appeared and slipped on his boots. "Now then, sir," he said.

"Alright, Tommy?" I asked.

"Champion, sir," he replied. "Except me back's killin' us with all that muck we've shifted." He nodded at the skip, brimming with soil and stones.

"Shut up moaning," said Bob. "It's character building, isn't it, Charlie?"

"Sure is," I confirmed.

"Just think how buff you'll look for all the birds," said Bob.

"Get fucked," he replied.

Bob just laughed. "You've got a mouth filthier than the town sewer," he said.

"Whatever," Tommy quipped. "When can we have a brew anyway?"

"Not yet," responded Bob and added, "you lazy sod, we've only been here 5 minutes. Finish putting those coping stones on that wall and we can have a brew then."

To my mind, it seemed that Bob and Tommy were getting on very well. Tommy certainly knew how to stand his own corner when it came to banter. I was even more confident that things would turn out well. Little was I to know how wrong I would be.

A few days later, I took a phone call from Bob. "Now then Bob, what can I do for you?" I said heartily.

"I've got a problem," he replied in rather a stern fashion. I didn't have time to respond but my positivity had evaporated at Bob's tone of voice so I stayed silent.

"I've just had a call from my customer at Great Siveton." He paused. "I don't quite get this but he was telling me that his house was burgled last night. Said they had taken all his wife's jewellery that was kept in their bedroom as well as some cash kept in a bedroom drawer."

"Bloody hell," I said. I was shocked.

"The thing is," he continued, "I had a call from my other customer in Manerton this morning, telling me the exact same thing."

"What?" I exclaimed.

"Yes, unfortunately, it looks like a bit of a coincidence doesn't it that I have 2 jobs and at both those jobs the houses have been burgled. Now I'm not accusing anyone but for the sake of my reputation, I have to look at all possibilities." He paused briefly and then continued, "In both cases, the customers have asked me to vouch for, and I quote 'The rough-looking youth with the potty mouth'. Under the circumstances, therefore, I have no choice but to let Tommy go."

"You're joking?" I pleaded. "There's no evidence that Tommy's done anything."

"I know, lad," he replied, "but I have to consider my reputation."

"How did the burglars get in?" I asked.

"Both owners have said the same thing," he replied, "that someone picked the lock on the back door and then went to get what they wanted from the house, almost as if they knew the layout of the place. I'm afraid I'll have to tell the police this information and also tell them about Tommy, so you better let him know that the police may be getting in touch."

"Wow," I said. I was lost for words; I had all sorts of things rushing through my mind. "Bob, I honestly don't know what to say but without evidence, I can't tell Tommy he's been sacked because he's a thief. I'll try and think of something to let him down gently."

"Sorry lad," he replied. "But as I say, it's my reputation."

Try to let Tommy down gently. I considered the thought of it. It was going to be impossible. The only thing I could think of doing was to be honest with him and he took the news as I expected, badly.

"Champion!" he exclaimed. "Bob's a fuckin' tool anyway. I wouldn't wanna work for 'im anymore. Full stop. I mean how am I supposed to get to Manerton or Great Siveton to nick owt? Fly? He's a bell end. It's got nowt to do wi' me so the coppers can get fucked n'all."

"I'm sorry," I said, trying to placate him. "I can always find you something else."

"Whatever," he said, his eyes darting here and there, his anger bouncing around like a mad cat in a sack.

"I mean where would I put the stuff?" he declared. "Fuckin' idiot."

"Look, Tommy," I said, "no one's accusing you of anything but Bob needs to protect his livelihood and we have to respect that, so a new placement will have to be found. And, if you've nothing to do with it, then the police won't find anything, will they?"

"Fuckin' coppers. Last time I had owt to do wi' them, a copper broke his leg tryin' to get me in t' cop car. Dick 'ead."

"Tommy, calm down yeah?" I pleaded with him. "I'm sure everything will come out in the wash. Like I say, if you've done nothing, then you've nothing to worry about."

"You reckon?" he replied. "Coppers will pin it on me anyway. They've been lookin' to pin summat on me for ages."

"Come on, Tommy, the police aren't going to frame a 16-year-old youth for a couple of burglaries."

"You don't know the coppers like I do, I fuckin' hate 'em," he said.

However, both Bob and Tommy were wrong in their summations. Firstly, there was no evidence that Tommy had been involved in a burglary. The police had questioned him extensively and verified his alibi. He had been at his girlfriend's house. Secondly, Tommy wasn't framed by the police, no matter how much his fertile imagination said they would. Over time, therefore, the whole affair drifted into insignificance, Tommy calmed down and we began to look for an alternative placement. Again I found Tommy a placement with a landscape gardening company but as a precaution, I advised them not to let Tommy into a customer's house. If he needed a wee, then he had to do it at the back of the garden or find a public toilet. Fortunately, they never asked why.

A few months passed and I was out doing my rounds as normal when my phone rang, it was Lauren.

"At last!" she said. "The house, it's ready!"

"Brilliant!" I replied with as much enthusiasm as hers. "I can't wait to move in."

"The lady who took us around the show home wants us to pop in to finalise the paperwork and discuss exchanging contracts," she said hastily. "Can you make it tomorrow morning?"

"Hold on, I'll check my diary," I said. I quickly flipped the phone so I could alter the screen to show my calendar. Having confirmed my suspicions, I answered back, "Yes, so long as we are done by 3 pm, I have to pick up Tommy Capstick from work."

"We'll be finished well before then. I can't wait!" And with that, she hung up.

The next morning we arranged to go around to the marketing suite at 10 am for our meeting to discuss the move. The lady in charge was called Sharon and she was shuffling through paperwork and looking rather flustered when we arrived.

"Is everything OK?" asked Lauren, obviously concerned that there may be a problem with our move.

"Oh yes, fine," she replied. "We just had an intruder last night and I was checking everything was still here."

"And?"

"Oh, er yes. It's all here," she said with relief.

"Intruder?" I asked.

"Yes, rather a funny thing actually," she replied. "I got to work as normal at about 8:30 this morning. The place was all locked up as you would expect, so when I got in, I put the kettle on and went to the loo. Unfortunately, there was no loo roll in the downstairs cloakroom so I went upstairs. Sorry for the detail but it's important."

Lauren and I just looked at one another and Sharon continued.

"As I got to the top of the stairs, I noticed there was someone or something asleep in the bed of the master bedroom. Well, when I saw that, I just screamed and this person or whatever jumped out of the bed like he was on fire. At that point, I ran downstairs and bumped into a couple of the lads from the building site coming the other way, as they had heard my screams." She paused.

"What happened then?" asked Lauren aghast.

"Well, the lads started to go upstairs slowly but were met by this figure hurtling towards them swearing like a trooper, so they let him past and he ran off outside and down the lane. It was quite bizarre."

"Did you call the police?" I asked.

"No, I didn't see the point, to be honest, as no one got a good look at him. Anyway, enough of that," she said, breaking into a huge smile. "Let's get on with your house move."

The meeting took an hour or so and left me plenty of time to do my rounds. I was on a real high knowing we would be in our new house in a few weeks. By 3 pm, I had almost forgotten the events of the morning and was pulling up outside a property with a new lawn and fencing as part of its garden renovation work. Tommy was waiting for me on the pavement.

"You alright," I said as he got into the car, immediately regretting it. I then suffered a 10-minute monologue about Tommy's ailments before he put his music on and drifted off into his own thoughts. That suited me, as I was quite happy to drift off into my own thoughts, dreaming of my new home.

"Fell out, wi' me bird last night!" he suddenly shouted. Christ I thought, I wasn't ready for that!

"Oh yeah?" I said.

"Fuckin' bitch," he exclaimed. "Just because I kicked her dog off the bed."

"Oh yeah?"

"Yeah, so she told me to fuck off. So, I told her to get fucked."

"How romantic," I quipped.

"Yeah right well, there was no point goin' 'ome as it was gone midnight, so you know them new houses down Badger Corner?"

"Yeah?"

"You know the ones wi' that massive show home?"

"Yeah?"

"Well, I slept in there last night. Broke in and slept in the big bed. I was so tired from workin' yesterday that I slept right through till this woman woke me up wi' 'er screaming'."

"Good God!"

"Aye, it was fuckin' hilarious. I was pissin' me knickers! I just run off as fast as I could."

As realisation dawned that Tommy's tales, although tall, may also be true, I had just one question for him.

"Tell me, Tommy," I said with trepidation, "how did you break in?"

"Oh, easy," he replied cockily. "I've got these skeleton keys that me uncle gave us when he went to prison. Works every time."

Dark Side of the Moon

"I don't believe it!" shouted Ibra. He was pacing around the office. "Oh! It's such a mess!"

"What's up?" I asked half-heartedly. I was used to Ibra's histrionics, bouncing from the top of the world and ending in a bottomless pit within moments. Though, one of his many positive qualities was his ability to not swear regardless of his distress.

"My car!" he moaned. "I was sat on the motorway in the slow lane in a traffic jam and a truck in the middle lane cut across me. This mmmmm…" He was struggling to keep his language clean. "Muppet! Yeah, muppet, pulled across and smashed my wing mirror off."

"I guess you're OK?" I asked.

"OK? I thought I was a goner!" he exclaimed.

"Is the car driveable?"

"Oh er, yeah, it's outside."

We went out together and had a look at it. The wing mirror had indeed gone but essentially, this was the only damage.

"It will polish out," I said in a friendly fashion. Ibra just glared; his eyes dark pools, his eyebrows knitted together in anger. He obviously didn't find it funny.

"I'm off to lie down in a darkened room," he said as gloomily as possible.

"Right," I said but Ibra was too busy feeling sorry for himself to care about anything I might say. He simply got up and headed in the direction of the print room, an old unused part of the building that rarely got the sun and would provide the perfect backdrop to his mood.

I also didn't have time to dwell on Ibra's problems as I had an appointment with a new student, and by sheer coincidence, I was also in a darkened room but not by choice.

It was dark, really dark. After being out in the bright sunlight, my eyes were struggling to adjust.

"He's upstairs in his room," said Mrs Fletcher. Apparently, Stephan wouldn't come downstairs as he practically lived in his bedroom. I duly went upstairs.

"Is there anyone there?" I asked into the darkness.

"Close the door!" barked a voice. I did, quickly. My vision was gone but my other senses were heightened, particularly my sense of smell and the odour was overpowering. One of unwashed bodies, clothes and bedding but no Febreze, thank God.

"Who is it?" came a voice somewhere to my left.

"Can I turn on the light?" I responded.

"No!" came the panicked reply as I stood on something which collapsed with a crash. It was a pile of plates and cutlery, glasses and mugs.

"Why not? I can't see a thing and I'm standing on stuff," I said with exasperation.

"Just keep moving forward," said the voice. "There's a chair about 2 metres from your left hand."

"I can't see it."

"Just keep walking slowly," said the voice. "It's there now."

I reached forward and felt the seat of the chair. My hand then moved to the arm of the chair and I slowly turned around to sit on it.

"Who are you?" said the voice again.

"I'm Charlie, I'm here to discuss work experience," I said. "Can we have some light?" He ignored me.

"Oh, yeah, mum said you were coming."

As my eyes adjusted to the gloom, I could see small chinks of light creeping past the curtains. I could also see that behind the curtains were blackout blinds that were taped at the edges to stop them from being drawn, although some of the tape was now peeling to let the light through. As my eyes adjusted a bit more to the gloom, the voice acquired a shape and then became the prone outline of a boy who was wearing a virtual reality headset. He turned to me slowly and removed it to reveal dark eyes and a pallid face, large ears and unkempt hair.

Stephan bore a close resemblance to a childhood friend I once had but the contrast in fortunes between him and my friend couldn't be starker.

My friend Ridge had a face that only a mother could love. Ears like dinner plates, a head as round as a pumpkin and a crop of mousy unkempt hair hanging over eyes that were too small for his face. He had lost his mum to cancer and had a father who spent his time grieving by playing golf and drinking in the local pubs and clubs. His dad was always out so his house became our impromptu gang hut. The house was also a treasure trove because in the front bedroom, there was no bed and no carpets, only curtains drawn to screen the treasure. Scattered in every corner and piled high on the floor were the latest trainers, sports clothes and sports equipment. There were golf clubs, cricket bats, cricket pads and balls. There were rugby balls, footballs, football boots and of course, trainers. Trainers to a teenager are like cocaine to a drug addict, a must-have accessory creating a burning lust for the latest fashion. Ridge had dozens of them. Puma G Villas, Adidas Samba's and Nike Tiempo football boots that Maradona wore.

Ridge's popularity grew as he began offering these items to all of us on terms similar to those offered by mail-order catalogues. We could pay weekly for our trainers and we could pay half the price these shoes were being sold at in the shops. We didn't ask any questions because we were the coolest kids because we had the coolest shoes. Shoes which shone like cats eyes through a fish bowl due to their reflective uppers.

We all loved to play sports and the fact that Ridge had every piece of equipment imaginable, meant we could play them in style. Our favourite was cricket, simply because it used the most equipment and therefore, meant that we were the envy of the other kids around us. If we weren't playing cricket we were playing golf and then as the days grew shorter and the nights longer, football and rugby. I even started to play badminton after buying a racket off Ridge, as my school had a new indoor sports hall and was starting a team. Over time, I made the school team and was even selected for Yorkshire. Unfortunately, I never played for the county team, as my parents didn't have a car and my dad spent my bus money in the company of Mr Ridge at the Top End club.

One summer's day, however, things changed. On the surface of it, it should have been catastrophic but it wasn't. Instead, it proved to be a defining moment in Ridge's life. It was the day his father went to prison.

I shook myself back to the present. "Do you mind taking the headset off, please Stephan?" I said. Slowly, he sat up and removed the helmet.

"I was enjoying that until you walked in," he responded.

"Well, I'm sorry but I refuse to talk to anyone who's unnecessarily distracted and I also refuse to talk to anyone who insists on living in absolute darkness," I continued.

"Jog on then," he said. "I'm not bothered about work experience anyway."

"Stephan," I said slowly, restraining myself, "let me put it this way. School have made it clear that they are not happy with your lack of attendance and they are not happy that you have holed yourself up in your bedroom, refusing to go out."

Just then the door opened slowly and in walked Mrs Fletcher. "What's that?" she inquired.

"I was just saying to Stephan that he needs to do work experience to improve his prospects and help him get out of the house."

"He's not doing any harm stopping in here," she replied.

"No maybe not, but it's not doing *him* any good, is it?" I said, turning to look at Stephan.

"What do you mean?" she asked her eyes following my gaze.

"Well basically, Stephan is in his final year of school and he is faced with a choice; employment, training or further education. What is not allowed is stopping at home, doing nothing and being a burden on the state," I said in a matter-of-fact manner.

"But he doesn't like school or going outside. It makes him feel anxious, doesn't it, Stephan?" she said.

"Yes, mum," he replied dutifully.

"He's always been sensitive. Even when he was little he wouldn't eat certain things, would you pet?" she continued. "He also struggled with making friends and I didn't want him playing out with some of the kids around here. They're too rough."

Stephan just sat there on his bed twiddling with the virtual reality headset in his hands. He was itching to get back to cyberspace.

Faced with such entrenched objections, I knew I was wasting my time but I wasn't giving up.

"Mrs Fletcher, I can see your concerns but he really doesn't have much of a choice, otherwise you could end up getting fined and Stephan could be permanently excluded resulting in a move to the Student Referral School."

Mrs Fletcher just stared at me for a moment. "Why can't you just leave us alone, we're not doing anyone any harm?"

"I've explained already Mrs Fletcher. Stephan can't live his life in this bedroom and if you want my opinion…"

"I'm not sure I do," she interjected.

"Well, I think I have a duty to offer it. The longer Stephan spends his time in here, the more anxious he will become about going outside, never mind getting a job," I said. Mrs Fletcher simply scowled as my frustration spilt over.

"I'm sorry, Mrs Fletcher, but you've wrapped this lad in cotton wool to the point that he has no social skills and no perception of reality."

"I'm not sure I like your tone, Mr Ryles," she said. "What do mean social skills? What reality!"

"What I mean is that in order to be of use to society, people looking for work need to have the skills to convince an employer to take them on."

"What's that got to do with social skills?"

"Simply, that if you have an ability to socialise with other young people and adults then you are more likely to have the confidence to put those skills into practice when meeting an employer. The reality is that there is a pressing need for Stephan to adjust to normal life as soon as he can."

"What's normal these days anyway?" she said. "He's happy and doing no one any harm. From what I can see, he's just a normal teenager."

I clearly wasn't making any progress, so I left the room and descended the stairs moving quickly to get into my car.

As I was driving back to the office, avoiding colliding with other vehicles or mounting the pavement and maiming pedestrians, I pondered how in contrast, Stephan would be doing the complete opposite.

Once back at the office, Ibra was waiting for me.

"£250," he said.

"For what?" I was still thinking about Stephan.

"Insurance excess for the wing mirror."

"Oh."

"I didn't get the truck's details, so I have to pay," he continued.

"Bad luck," I offered.

"Mmm. So where've you been today?" he asked.

"Seeing this young lad who won't come out of his bedroom," I replied. "Just sits there in the dark playing computer games."

I paused. "Which reminds me, did you have fun in the print room?"

Ibra glared at me with his piercing eyes. "Are you taking the proverbial?"

"Sorry, I couldn't resist!" I laughed.

"Thing is though, this kid is the spitting image of an old friend of mine from when I was a kid," I continued.

"How can you tell when it's dark?" Ibra chuckled to himself. He was back to his old self once more.

"Funny bugger!" I said and continued. "But he does, he's his twin. He'd not had the best start in life either but he was a very resourceful kid in contrast to the layabout I saw earlier."

"Are you going back to see him?" he asked.

"Yes, tomorrow," I replied. "I've got to try and get this lad to engage and maybe my old childhood friend could have some lessons for him if he wants to listen."

I could see it on Ibra's face 'here we go again'. He had the patience for a bit of banter but not a full-blown story about a childhood friend, so I simply eased back into my chair and kept my thoughts to myself.

The following day, I was back at Stephan's house. "Can you take the headset off please?" I asked. I didn't believe I would achieve anything by going to see him again but I was there to help the school as much as I could. He slowly unclipped the equipment from his head and blinked at the light in the room. I had deliberately left the bedroom door open so I could see his dishevelled face.

"Thank you," I offered. "Like last time, I'm looking to see what type of work experience would suit you."

"I don't want to do work experience," he replied simply.

"You don't really have a choice," I said.

"Will I get paid?" he asked.

"No, I'm afraid, as it is part of an alternative to the school curriculum."

"I'm not doing it then," he said.

"Why not?" I asked and continued. "What have you got to offer any employer that would deserve payment?"

"I could be an influencer," he responded.

"A what?" I asked in disbelief. I really didn't have a clue what he was talking about and he could see the confusion on my face.

"An influencer," he continued in a patronising fashion, "is someone who gets thousands and thousands of followers on the internet."

"And what would you influence them about?"

"Don't know yet. I'll have to think about it," he said.

"If you don't mind me saying so, you've had plenty of time to think about it stuck in this bedroom," I said.

"Well, that's what I want to be," he said.

"I'm sorry, Stephan, but you must be more realistic. You can't do work experience as an influencer," I replied. "Can't you think of something else?"

"No. I want to be an influencer, making YouTube videos."

Just then Mrs Fletcher came up the stairs.

"Well?" she asked.

"It seems Stephan wants to be an influencer," I told her.

"A what?" she replied, so Stephan explained what it was to her.

"Seems reasonable to me," she said. "Why can't you find him a job like that?"

"Firstly, it's the type of job that someone builds for themselves and normally, they tend to have a talent making videos," I said. "And secondly, it keeps Stephan firmly rooted in his bedroom. It certainly doesn't tackle the issues he faces in going out and spending time with other people in a working environment."

"Well," she said, "he wants to be an influencer, so if you can't find him a job like that then I can't see what else there is to say."

"That's a shame, Mrs Fletcher," I replied. "Because if you are determined to ignore my advice then I will have to go back to school and let them know what's happened. I can't help feeling that you are going to end up in trouble and probably attract even more attention to Stephan's situation. I can't emphasise enough what the consequences might be."

She just looked at me and half shifted her body to allow me to step out of the room so I obliged gratefully. Neither she nor Stephan were in any mood to hear about Ridge and how he'd handled the problems in his life and I wasn't going to force that story on them but they might have learned something from it.

We'd had a fun afternoon playing cricket but we had to wrap up the game a little early after a fierce shot had seen the ball disappear in the long grass. No bother as we had dozens of replacements in Ridge's front bedroom.

As we wandered back, the sun was warm on our backs and we were looking forward to having a cool drink back at Ridge's house. However, as Ridge put the key in the door to let us all in, he noticed that the door was in fact unlocked.

Nudging it slowly, he hefted the cricket bat in his hand and entered the house with the rest of us following closely behind. It was clear that there was no one downstairs, so Ridge, armed with his bat, climbed up to the bedrooms.

"We've been robbed!" he shouted suddenly.

"What!" came the collective reply as we fought each other to get up the stairs. Soon enough, we could see the cause of his angst, the front bedroom was totally empty. Not a bat, ball, shoe box or golf club remained.

As we stared in awe at the large empty space, there was a loud authoritative shout from downstairs.

"Andrew Ridgeley. Is that you upstairs?"

"Who the hell is that?" whispered Ridge to the group. We offered a collective shrug.

"Andrew Ridgeley, can you come downstairs please, I have some important news for you," shouted the voice.

As we descended the stairs, we saw black shiny boots appear, leading to black trousers, a blazer and then a policeman's head.

"Sorry I missed you, I was in the back garden. I needed to pay a call," he said.

"What do you want?" said Ridge. The policeman ignored him.

"You lot, I want your names and then you can clear off home," he said. Duty done, we sloped off slowly.

A couple of days later, there was a knock on the door. Mum answered and stood there in the doorway was the same copper.

"Are you Charlie Ryles' mum?" he asked.

"Yes," replied mum. "What's he done?"

"I don't know yet. Can I have a word with him? I'm PC Sykes by the way."

"Yes. Come in, officer, he's watching TV," she replied and showed him into the living room where I was sitting.

"Turn that off," he said. I did as I was told even though the A-Team was on the set, blowing up the baddies but no one ever got killed. I never understood that.

He looked at my feet. "Where did you get those trainers?" he asked.

"I bought them off Ridge," I replied.

"Where did he get them?" he enquired.

"I have no idea," I responded. I really did not have a clue other than his dad got them from work. PC Sykes continued his questions, always returning to the central question as to where Mr Ridgeley had got the trainers from and all the while I answered honestly. I really didn't know.

"What's going on, officer?" My mum eventually asked.

"I don't see telling you doing any harm," he said. "Basically, Ravensdeal Sports is a large manufacturer and importer of sports equipment based on the other side of town and unfortunately, the firm has seen quite a lot of its stock being stolen over quite a period of time. Having looked into it, it seems that most of this stock has ended up on the feet of local teenagers like Charlie."

Mum gave me an evil stare as PC Sykes continued.

"Unfortunately, one of these teenagers was the son of one of my colleagues who took him to buy some trainers from Mr Ridgeley. Suspecting something was wrong, we gained a warrant to enter the house and found a large collection of sports equipment in Mr Ridgeley's front bedroom. Having removed the goods, we then arrested Mr Ridgeley and found that he has worked for Ravensdeal Sports for the last 5 years."

"So what's this got to do with Charlie?" she asked.

"Nothing," he said, "other than being in possession of stolen goods. However, considering that they are in no condition to be returned, he may as well keep them. Anyway, I've got a lot of kids to see, so I'll get on my way." And with that, he promptly stood up.

"I'll see myself out," he said and with that, he left.

Mr Ridgeley was sent to prison for 6 months but nothing really changed for Ridge. What I hadn't realised was that he was already very capable of looking after himself. Since their mum had died and dad had started drinking, he was forced to cook his own meals, clothe himself and keep the house clean. By necessity, he had become very adept at it. Although dad was now in prison, which would derail most teenagers, it didn't affect Ridge, he just carried on as normal like nothing had happened. In fact, now that Andrew was 16, he was allowed to stay at home and avoided going into care so long as there was another responsible adult around. That responsible adult was his aunt May who lived miles away but offered the pretence of looking after and supporting him, even though this was a paper exercise. For all intents and purposes, he was allowed to look after himself, doing his own shopping, gardening, paying the bills, whatever was needed. Thus, life continued as normal for him and the rest of us, other than our supply of new trainers had dried up. What he did miss out on however was the love and support of a parent but he seemed to cope OK without his dad.

When Mr Ridgeley came out of prison, however, things did change. He no longer had a job and was therefore spending more time at home than usual, so our gang hut was no longer accessible and by default, Ridge wasn't the popular kid he used to be. I still saw him from time to time but he was by now working as a kitchen fitter's apprentice and he had money in his pocket and an eye for a bargain, so he already had a cheap run-around to drive when he turned 17. That eye for a bargain must have come from the forced period of household budgeting when his dad was in prison and Ridge was an expert. Before long, he had changed his job and was working in the household clearance business, emptying properties left by deceased relatives whose families didn't want the hassle of sorting through their belongings and disposing of the furniture. I never thought it would make him rich but at least it played to his strengths.

Looking back on that time, I get a real sense of how resilient and independent he was and by comparison how dependent Stephan is on his mother. There are now recognised disorders around social anxiety that would explain Stephan's behaviour but these are first-world problems. Ridge didn't have the luxury of being anxious, he had a household to run and he had to face his responsibilities whereas these days, a young man of 15 isn't forced to face his responsibilities to the same degree. Stephan can't even leave his bedroom and he probably doesn't even know which end of an iron to hold, never mind make himself presentable and keep up a pretence to avoid social services intervention like Ridge did. The key to success in these circumstances is that parents believe that work experience is the best way of engaging their child in a worthwhile activity. It is the first tentative step in helping them become independent. Sadly, Mrs Fletcher didn't believe that it was as she felt the best way of helping her son was to keep him wrapped tightly in cotton wool. Stephan's journey through life is therefore likely to be a difficult one, peppered with constant anxiety, under constant scrutiny and even under the pain of financial penalties for his mum.

Ibra and I were going through our weekly ritual of student updates with a constant stream of "sacked", "in bed" and "sick" ringing in our ears.

"What about Stephan?" asked Ibra.

"No change. Still stuck in his blacked-out bedroom." I then proceeded to bring Ibra up to speed on progress and how it made me think of Ridge. Now that Ibra's car had been fixed, he was much calmer and had listened keenly to my story and even had some advice.

"Why don't you check him out on social media?" he said. "We do it for all our students and parents, why not check out your old mate?"

"That's a good idea!" I replied and with a bit of careful guesswork and snooping, I eventually found him.

"Look at this," I said a few days later. "Remember Ridge?" Ibra nodded. "You won't believe this, he's now living in Spain in a big house on the Costa Del Sol."

"Who's that?" asked Ibra, drawn to the pretty woman in Ridge's arms.

"That's his missus," I replied. "He's also got 3 kids as well and he seems to be running a very successful haulage hire business. The thing is I can't work out how he made such a large amount of money. Any questions I ask of other friends only offer rumours and innuendo."

"A proper rogue eh?"

"Could be because when I piece the various bits together, it looks like he took over a house clearance business having acquired a large windfall. It's rumoured the money came from selling second-hand jewellery that never made it into the company register, moreover, the suggestions are they ended up in his pocket. However, it seems that once he had taken over the business, he then expanded into hiring commercial vans out to other tradesmen as a sideline. This business eventually became his main enterprise which allowed him to employ men of a certain character to collect the hire payments. These 'collections' sometimes involved personal property when cash wasn't available, which fed straight into the furniture disposals business he still owned. Ridge had become a good old-fashioned mobster and his enterprise eventually went international with his move to the continent."

"Wow," exclaimed Ibra. "A proper, full-on Costa Del criminal!"

"It certainly shows what you can achieve in life if you're clever enough," I replied. "In contrast, young Stephan has learnt nothing about life sitting in his bedroom."

"Who says crime doesn't pay," declared Ibra. "This guy has more fingers in more pies than the guy who owns Greggs."

I chuckled because there is one final key lesson that stands out for me regarding Stephan Fletcher that Ridge learnt extremely well at the age of 16. That lesson is that if you want to influence people and make money from them, then you also need to know how not to get caught, particularly, if you have no intention of following the rules.

Every Breath You Take

I was travelling to meet Ibra to discuss our progress when I came across a police speed trap and sure enough, there he was again. It was the same police officer almost hidden behind a tree at the centre of the village green, gun in hand, waiting for the unsuspecting speeding driver to pass by. It was a relief to note that I was doing a steady 30 mph and safe in that knowledge, a smug grin appeared on my face. I could almost see him slump in disappointment. This particular officer had caught me three times previously. On the first occasion, I was eligible for a speed awareness course, unfortunately, on the next two occasions, I had to pay a fine and accrue points on my driving licence.

Both Ibra and I had points on our licence, an inevitable occupational hazard of doing 30,000 miles a year travelling in and out of towns and villages with varying and sometimes unfathomable speed limits. They say that regular lamp posts dictate 30 mph but not in Yorkshire. There are stretches of national speed limit with street lighting and no repeater signs and there are 20-mile zones that are poorly outlined and various other oddities. Not that I'm bitter but considering the crimes my students get up to, it should be a crime to punish those trying to help them.

Ibra has nine points and suffices to say he drove like a church vicar on his way to a funeral. He was terrified that if he got another three points he could have his licence revoked. Although it could have serious ramifications to lose his licence, it didn't stop me from provoking him whenever I could. On that day, Ibra and I had agreed to meet at a roadside café. Typically, I was there at least 20 minutes before he turned up.

"You took your time," I teased. He dropped into the seat opposite me, closing his body like an open umbrella sliding into its stand. He stared.

"You should be driving a Honda Jazz, Ibra," I continued. "You'd feel right at home tripping between the doctors and the garden centre."

"Very funny," he retorted. "The thing is, though, I've only got another two months before I go back to six points so I can take whatever you throw at me."

"Yes, mate but it could be a long two months, particularly driving a car with only two gears." I chuckled.

He raised an eyebrow. "Shall we just get on with it?" he said. "Because you've got six points on your licence and all it would take would be for you to get caught daydreaming and you'll be driving like you've got all day like I have to."

"Sure mate," I replied. "Just don't take as long updating me on your students as you did getting here."

We spent the next half an hour going through our student roll, with all the typical scenarios playing out. We had become so immune to surprises that we almost accepted them as part of the job. In one example, Ibra told me of one particular lad who had fallen out with the owner of a garage where he was working, so he had threatened to burn the garage down. The owner of the garage took this threat very seriously as the young lad was from a notorious family that tended to resolve disputes in this sort of fashion. In the end, the young lad didn't set fire to the place but he was removed from the project for safeguarding reasons.

Having finished our meeting, I resolved to go back a different way to avoid the speed trap but as is his want, the officer had moved and was waiting by the phone box in Bassethall village on my alternative route, just as the speed limit changes to a 30. Fortunately, I saw him and made sure I was doing the correct speed. I was really starting to dislike this chap, I'd been caught three times and had seen him twice on the same day, I was starting to imagine he was trying to catch me again and I was convinced he recognised my car.

Once through Bassethall, I relaxed into my journey. I was on my way to see Tommy Capstick, the potty-mouthed lout working with a landscape gardener. Fortunately, no more burglaries had occurred and Tommy was continuing to avoid the law or retribution for his misdemeanours, although his stories were still colourful and full of inaccuracies and exaggerations as before. Or were they? I never really trusted what was or wasn't the truth when it came to Tommy.

As normal, he was waiting for me outside the property being renovated.

"Jump in, Tommy," I said.

"Alright, sir?" he asked.

"Not too bad, Tom," I replied. "I've just managed to avoid getting a speeding ticket so I'm not going to go via Bassethall if that's OK."

"It's alright with me, sir. Fucking coppers," he declared stretching his arms.

"Are you OK?" I asked. DOH! Here we go.

"Knackered!" he said. "Just been put on some new pills for me ADHD." He yawned loudly and snorted his nose, swallowing the phlegm.

"Oh yeah," I said feeling a bit queasy.

"They've stopped me shaking like a shitting dog but I can't sleep," he moaned. "Tek this morning, right? I'd been staring at the ceiling for hours when my mum said it was time to get up for work."

"Right."

PFFFFT. He opened a can of caffeine drink. "Man, I'm fucking shattered!" He took a large gulp of the orange-coloured liquid, put his earphones in and started listening to his music, rocking rhythmically to the beat. I drove on.

"What the fuck!" he shouted loudly.

"What?" I replied in a panic.

"Back there was a car stuck on its roof in a field, you best turn back."

"Where?"

"Before the corner. Looks like it's in a right mess. No one will walk out of that."

I really was worried about his reaction so I turned around as quickly as I could and we went back the way we had come. Sure enough, just after the corner a car had burst through a dry stone wall and had ended up on its roof.

By some small miracle, standing beside the car looking extremely dazed was a young lad. We quickly jumped out of the car.

"Are you OK?" I asked him.

"Eh?" he replied.

"Hey up, Robbie." Tommy chuckled. "Been robbing cars again?"

"Eh?"

"It's Robbie Marston, sir, a right rogue. One of my mates!"

"Have you called the police?"

"Urrgh!"

"Do you need an ambulance?"

"Urrghh!" Clearly, Robbie was in a bit of a mess. I, therefore, called 999 and requested both the police and ambulance service. I then checked the vehicle for other occupants and leaking fuel. This was particularly important as there was a child's seat in the back.

"Did you have a child in the back?" I asked him urgently.

"Err."

"A child. In the back!" I repeated.

"Err, err no. No kid."

"Thank God for that," I declared. Just then, both Tommy and I heard a police siren but I felt a huge wave of relief pass over me, Tommy looked like he was about to run. It was a police motorcycle and I could see as it got nearer that it was the police officer who had been manning the speed trap in Bassethall.

He pulled up, dismounted and rushed over to us. "Robbie Marston?" he asked. "Is that you?" He looked over him and sensing he wasn't in immediate danger called in to the base with the registration plate of the car.

Receiving the information he was expecting, he addressed Robbie once more. "Have you been borrowing other people's stuff again, Robbie?" Without waiting for a reply, he noticed

Tommy standing next to me trying to look innocent. His eyes were fixed on the ground.

"And if it isn't Tommy Capstick," he said. "You look remarkably well Tommy considering the state of that car."

"Nothing to do with me, you pig! I was with him," he replied with indignation, nodding in my direction.

"No need for that young man. If you don't want to be arrested, you'll curb your tongue!" He then looked at me.

"Oh," he said, "it's you."

I knew he was after me!

"And you are?"

"Charlie Ryles, officer," I replied. "And yes, Tommy was with me."

"How so?" he enquired.

"I help students find work experience placements to keep them out of trouble and I had just collected Tommy from work to take him home, when Tommy spotted the car on its roof," I replied. He looked ruefully at Tommy. I imagine he would have also suffered Tommy's tall tales during his dealings with him.

"Very commendable," he said. I was a bit taken aback.

"What is?" I asked.

"Work experience. What you do for these kids, it's a really good idea."

"Oh, thanks."

"They need as much support as they can get to keep them out of trouble. I have a lot of respect for people like you, prepared to take them on."

Tommy just stood there fidgeting; I assumed the caffeine was coursing through his veins in an adrenaline rush. Just then an ambulance screamed around the corner and pulled up behind the PC's motorbike. They came over to us and asked various questions of the police officer before they took over the care of Robbie. Police Officer Scarbrook, as he was called, then spent a few minutes making sure the traffic was moving safely past the parked vehicles before sorting out the details of the incident with us. And as the ambulance left, we also spent a few minutes swapping anecdotes of our experiences with the young reprobates in the district. He was a very likeable and affable man and I had totally changed my opinion of him.

"Nice bloke that," I said to Tommy as we set off for his home once more.

"He's an absolute bastard!" he replied. "He's still gonna shop Robbie for stealing that motor."

"And so he should," I replied indignantly. "There was a kiddie's seat in that car. Clearly, a young family used that car as a run-a-round. What will they do now?"

"I dunno." He shrugged. "Why should I give a fuck?"

There's no helping some people, I thought.

A few days later, PC Scarbrook rang to confirm that Robbie had been charged with stealing the car, and apart from a few bruises was in good physical health.

"What will he get?" I asked.

"Probably a custodial sentence I should imagine, as he's done it before," he replied. "It's a shame he hadn't been on your project, as I must admit, I've not seen a lot of Tommy Capstick lately, which is a good thing!" I blanched slightly as I thought about the burglaries a few months before.

"Anyway, I must get on, I've got my rounds to do," he said and with that, he hung up.

Tommy was incandescent with rage when he found out Robbie was likely to be incarcerated for stealing the car and he took great pleasure in gesticulating and swearing each time we passed a police car, or police officer when we were driving around. It always caught me unawares as he was usually deep in thought listening to his music when it happened.

Over the next few weeks, I was busy meeting parents, students and employers and didn't come across PC Scarbrook at all on my rounds. Then one day, I was driving into Bassethall once more when I saw him by the phone box with his speed gun. Without thinking, I waved and received a very cheery wave in return and I continued on my way. He really was a nice bloke.

It was another couple of weeks after that when Ibra and I were in the office doing our regular catch-up. Ibra was in a good mood for a change and had even offered to get the coffees.

"You're happy with yourself," I said.

"Yup," he said. "Number one, I've lost three points off my licence, so I'm back on six and number two, all my students are behaving themselves at the moment so I've managed to get to the gym more often."

"Lucky you," I said.

"Not luck, Charlie. Skill," he quipped, "skill."

"Oh, I nearly forgot." He rummaged through some things on his desk. "You've got a letter from York."

"What is it?" I asked.

"I don't know," he said. "Do you want me to open it?"

"You might as well," I replied. "It's probably a bill."

With that, Ibra proceeded to open the letter and remove the papers inside. I saw his eyebrows rise quickly and a look of sheer joy appeared on his face.

"Ha, Ha!" he said. "Can you believe it?"

"What is it?" I asked with urgency. "Has someone paid a bill?"

"Oh no," he replied. "It's better than that."

"Well?"

"Serves you right, my old mate," he said passing over the letter.

"What are you on about?" I said taking it off him and scanning the pages.

"You've got a speeding fine," he said in triumph. "You were doing 37mph in a 30 zone in Bassethall village two weeks ago!"

"Bloody hell!" I said and the thought suddenly struck me that maybe Tommy Capstick was right.

PC Scarbrook is an absolute b*stard!

Sugar, Honey

"Sugar, love?"

"No, thanks," I replied. No hospitality, you just don't know what you might catch.

"Don't mind if I have one, do you?" responded Mrs Blakely.

"No, you go ahead," I said. I was standing just outside the kitchen in a grubby hallway, struggling to see what Mrs Blakely was doing in the kitchen. To my right was the living room and the door was ajar. It had a conspicuous depression about two-thirds of the way up to where someone had punched it, possibly in frustration. Beyond the door, I could see into the room where there were two sofas opposite each other and gathered underneath were the detritus of discarded food, cob-webs, dust, dog hair and lego. Between the sofas was a bare floor of cheap laminate that had an unusually clean rectangle approximately 8ft by 4ft in shape. Around, it the patina was like the surface of a chain smoker's fingers, whereas inside the rectangle, the floor shone like a mirror but with a surface akin to an ice rink after a dance-off. The clue to why there were so many scratches was barking furiously in the back garden having been put there for my safety, and as I looked further around the room, it was obvious the dog spent a lot of time scrabbling around on the floor and jumping up at the windows. Everywhere was scratched, chewed or grubby from the dog's attention.

"Go on in, love, and sit down," said Mrs Blakely. I jumped at the sound of her voice and tentatively entered the room. The smell would have been horrendous but was even worse due to the lingering and cloying odour of Febreze. I gagged because I had spent far too much time in its company.

"Sorry about the floor, the dog ate the rug. Chewed it to chuffing bits, little sod. I was just in the middle of cleaning up when you arrived," she said almost absent-mindedly.

I ignored her, noticing the vacuum cleaner left conspicuously in the middle of the room but also noticing the raft of bite marks along the length of the cord. The vacuum cleaner probably hadn't been used in months. I tried to find somewhere to perch so that if required, I could take flight at any moment. In vain, I searched for a relatively clean patch of cloth on the sofa but to no avail. I, therefore, sat on the wooden arm of the sofa or rather leant on it. In my mind, this was a good plan as it was too small for the dog to lie on. However, I didn't account for the splinters due to the dog chewing on it like a large bone, one of which slid into my buttocks as I rested my weight. I sprang back like a jack-in-the-box. Mrs Blakely just gawped at me as my face twisted in pain.

"Sit down love, just there." She pointed at the seat nearest the window, the one with a decidedly disgusting smell. "Chuck all the papers on the floor or somewhere."

I resigned myself to sit down, rubbing my rear, searching for a conspicuous splinter or patch of blood. I then felt for the sofa and discovered that the cloth had a decidedly greasy feel.

Faced with this, I made my mind up to strip off as soon as I got home and throw my clothes into the washing machine on the hottest cycle. Once my clothes were being disinfected, I would then have a shower, followed by a bath filled with Lysol and Cif; extreme but effective.

After what seemed like an age, the pain subsided and I eventually composed myself to a point where I could begin to ease myself onto the edge of the grubby seat and explain what we did, namely help young people find work experience and in this case, I would be helping her son Thomas.

"I thought Thomas would be here," I said.

"He is. He's upstairs in his pit. I'll give him a shout," she said. She then took a breath. "… THOMAS!"

There was a muffled reply from above.

"Get your arse down here now. That bloke from work experience wants to talk to you!"

I involuntarily screwed my eyes shut at the sound of Mrs Blakely's voice but like any consummate professional, quickly composed myself without her noticing.

There then followed a prolonged silence until eventually, Thomas entered the room wearing a well-worn track suit, odd socks and no shoes. At least the floor would get a polish, I mused.

"Sit down over there," barked Mrs Blakely at her son. Thomas shuffled next to me. "No! Not there, THERE!" She pointed at the floor by the fireplace. Thomas sat where he was told.

"Daft bugger he is," she said. "Right love. You were saying."

I leant forward as far as I dare to ensure as little of my posterior was touching the sofa and began to explain why I was there. Things proceeded with difficulty as Mrs Blakely interjected regularly to admonish her son and then to politely ask me to continue.

I took in my surroundings and was expecting to hear a tale of broken relationships, neglect, and disinterest in school as well as tales of disruptiveness, spells in isolation and exclusion from school. What he heard instead was that Mr and Mrs Blakely were very hard working, with her working as a dinner lady at the local primary school, as well as cleaning at the local office block on an evening, and Mr Blakely working as a long-distance lorry driver. But it was still true that Thomas had spent most of his educational career in isolation or temporary exclusion due to his total lack of interest in being there. It was now obvious to me that Mr and Mrs Blakely spent so little time at home that they didn't have the ability to supervise Thomas who consequently spent a lot of time lounging in bed and watching TV. And neither did they have the motivation to clean up. The house was very much like the aftermath of a teenagers' party in a squat.

I had seen this kind of situation before. Parents are so busy holding it all together that routine can collapse but at least I knew that Thomas was likely to engage well with the program. He may have seemed to be lazy but actually, he needed to be inspired and motivated and there was something in our conversation that gave me some confidence and an idea of what to do to help him.

The one thing that the family did do to try and help make ends meet was to grow their own vegetables. Being September, they had an abundance of potatoes, cabbages, carrots and onions, as well as blackberries, raspberries, gooseberries and apples. It seemed that as much as Thomas liked his bed, he also enjoyed being in the allotment at the back of the house, the place where the dog was now, safely out of the way. As it barked furiously, I had this image of a huge wolf or even bear, salivating at the prospect of getting hold of me and gnawing on my flesh and bones relentlessly as if I was his supper.

I left the Blakely's home with a palpable sense of relief. I hadn't been mauled by the dog but on the other hand, I was longing for a wash. Later that evening, lying in a deep hot bath, I started to develop a plan as to what to do next regarding Thomas and his work experience. My plan was to approach the local council Parks and Gardens department to see if we could build on Thomas's interest in horticulture and find him a placement working with plants.

It took some time, due to the bureaucracy of working with a government body, but after an initial phone call and then emails and meetings, health and safety briefings and box-ticking, the local council eventually offered to take Thomas on. Result! The only thing now was to go back to see the family and talk through the details. Unfortunately, this brought back a few unpleasant memories and thinking about my last visit, I made an involuntary scratch at my posterior.

I went through the same routine, perched on the same seat with Thomas sat by the fireplace in the hope I could come out of the meeting relatively clean.

"Oh it's grand," declared Mrs Blakely. "Our Thomas, working for the council!" She beamed across at me like I was the saviour himself. She continued.

"Ah don't know how to thank you, young man. Do we, Thomas? Know how to thank him!" She glared at Thomas.

"Thanks," said Thomas.

"We can do better than that," she said. "I'll be back in a minute!"

Thomas and I stayed where we were in silence while she disappeared out of the room. Before long, she returned with a large wooden box, the type you see on market stalls, filled to the brim with fresh vegetables.

"Here lad," she said beaming again. "Have these."

I was genuinely taken aback. Of all the kindness that can be offered in this world, the one gift that is most precious is that which is given by those who can't afford it. It's fine for celebrities to donate thousands, if not millions of pounds to charity or even set up a charity in their own name but they do not offer the kind of charity that someone with everything to lose does.

"I can't take these," I said. "I just can't."

I knew full well that the Blakely s were living on the edge of poverty, working in low-paid jobs to maintain their household. More than likely their vegetable patch gave them the opportunity to fund a few luxuries that most of us take for granted.

"No lad, I won't have it," she said. "Our Thomas has a job with the council. He's going up in the world."

"Hold on a second, Mrs Blakely," I replied. "All I've done is organise work experience for Thomas. He's not going to be paid and it's not permanent. It's simply work experience."

"Don't be so modest, lad, I can see what this is," she continued. "It's a chance for our Thomas to get a career if he sticks with it. Take them lad, with my blessing."

I looked at the vegetables in their brown box. Fresh and bursting with vitality, they were covered in earth, freshly hewn from the soil. There wasn't a more humble or more precious gift in the world.

"Thank you," I said simply. Mrs Blakely sat back into her chair with a triumphant smile and winked in Thomas's direction.

"If you're happy then, I'll get on my way," I said and with that, I stood up with the bulging gift in my arms. Without thinking, I reached my full height and stepped onto the lighter patch of polished and scratched lino. At that moment, I felt my leg shift forward under a weight I had totally underestimated. I had 15 kg of vegetables pivoting me forward, trying to hurl me onto the floor. With a rising panic, I realised I was doing the splits. I knew I didn't have the flexibility for that and would lock up before titling sideways into the grime and filth of the floor.

In horror, I tipped forward slowly trying to balance the vegetables, for now they had the value of the crown jewels and nothing was going to make me let go of them. I would sacrifice my dignity to keep them in the box and stop then cascading out and under the sofa, never to be seen again. With relief, I felt a hand under my arm.

"Come here!" said Mrs Blakely, hoisting me up. "Where were you going then?" she said.

I looked into her eyes with gratitude from under my furrowed brow but then felt the vice-like grip of Mrs Blakely on my arm. Her fingers were like pincers. I now had a piercing pain from being held like the shaft of a collier's spade but I was still upright and tentatively felt the lino in front of me for grip.

"Thank you," I said again. I sounded pathetic. I wasn't used to being manhandled by a pocket battleship like Mrs

Blakely. Slowly but surely, one step at a time, I eventually made it out of the room and into the street.

"Thank you," I said again weakly. I gingerly put the vegetables into the back of the car and once the front door of the house had closed with Mrs Blakely disappearing behind it, I rubbed my arm profusely trying to rid myself of the pain, only to see Thomas laughing like a jackal in the window of the front room.

With no further appointments, I drove back to the office and found Ibra at his desk typing up some case notes. "What's up with you?" he asked, raising just one eyebrow. "You look like you've got a bit of a sweat on."

"I have," I replied. "I've just been to sort a placement out for a student and because his mum was so grateful, I'd found one she gave me a box full of home-grown vegetables."

"Why the sweat though?" he asked again.

"Well," I replied, "apart from the box being very heavy, it almost crippled me as I tried to manoeuvre my way out of the house. The lino was like an ice rink and I slipped."

"Ha!" He laughed. "Did you nearly get a face full of house fluff and skanky tapas?" I scowled at him. "Thinking about it though," he continued, "there must be a lot of veg in that box. Can I have some?"

Ibra was a vegetarian and the idea of eating home-grown vegetables would have been very tempting for him. He was very body-conscious, keeping fit with his boxing and watching carefully what he ate.

"You can have the lot if you want," I offered.

"You sure?" he said.

"Yeah no problem, you'll get more out of them than I will," I replied.

Ibra wasn't the most patient individual and we were quickly transferring the box of vegetables from my car to his. All the while his eyes were glistening with the prospect of creating new culinary delights.

Over the coming weeks, the vegetables made their way into soups and pies as well as accompaniments to various meals. Ibra declared that they were delicious.

"Only made more delicious by the fact that they were home-grown and that they were a precious gift willingly offered." He would say in a jaunty fashion.

The other positive was that Thomas was doing a fabulous job for the council. He worked in the grass cutting team; he worked building borders, planters and hedgerows. He also carried out the mulching and composting as he went. Throughout the year, Thomas had worked for various supervisors and managers and had impressed to the point where the council were prepared to offer him an apprenticeship. Towards the end of May, I received an email from Paul Dick, the Parks and Gardens Manager, inviting him and Thomas to a meeting, ostensibly to discuss progress.

Thomas and I arrived on time and were ushered into a shabby office last decorated in the 1980 s. All the furniture was brown velour and the desks dark wooden affairs that would take a fork lift truck to move.

After five minutes or so, a man in bright high viz clothing entered the room and introduced himself.

"Call me Dave," he said. I looked puzzled.

"I thought we were meeting Paul?"

"Don't worry," said Dave. "I am Paul but there are three Paul s that work here. Me, Peter and Paul."

"Who's Peter?" I asked, confused.

"Paul McShane," he replied. "Can't get confused then."

"Right," I replied, even more confused so I changed the subject. "How's Thomas getting on?"

"Thomas?" It was Dave's turn to look puzzled.

"Which Thomas?"

"Thomas Blakely, the student I placed on work experience. That Thomas." I nodded in the student's direction. My confusion was tilting into frustration and I began perspiring slightly. I moved to stretch my legs and place my arms behind my head.

"Oh that Thomas!" exclaimed Dave. "I was only joking! However, we call him Deano."

"OK?" I said losing the plot even more.

"Well, yes," said Dave as breezily as he could. "Just having a laugh with you. We've already got a Thomas so we call him Deano as we don't have one of them and may I say Deano's done a top job working for us. So good that we want to offer him an apprenticeship from September."

My frustration evaporated in an instant.

"An apprenticeship! That's fantastic! What do you think of that Thomas, er Deano?" I asked.

"Sick!" he said excitedly.

Now Dave looked confused. "Sick?"

"Yeah, mega! My mum's gonna be well chuffed!" he continued.

"Look, Mr Dick," I said.

"Dave, please," said Dave. "Call me Dave."

"Dave…" I replied, pausing somewhat. "This is fantastic! We… the school… Tho… er… Deano here, I mean what a brilliant outcome. I can't thank you enough."

Everyone shook hands and we left the room on cloud nine. Deano and I jumped into the car parked outside and drove straight to Deano's house. No sooner had we arrived and had begun walking up the garden path, when the barking began, like a growling bear getting louder and louder.

"Just wait there, I'll move the dog," advised Deano as he opened the door. I stayed in the garden.

"Oh for God's sake, Ben!" shouted Deano at the dog. All I could hear next was a dog being dragged over the lino, a door slamming and the dog's barks echoing from the allotment at the back.

"Come in," said Deano. "But be careful. Dog's shit is all over the floor in the room."

"I'll wait here if you don't mind," I said politely as I could. Deano went back inside and started spraying something into the living room with liberal abandon. Then suddenly the living room window sprang open with a crash and out billowed the odour of dog mess and Febreze. Suddenly, I felt the urge to retch.

Then without warning, Mrs Blakely appeared at the garden gate.

"What's up?" she said.

I didn't hesitate. "Deano, er Thomas had got an apprenticeship with the council."

"Fantastic!" she bellowed. "Oh, how can I thank you?"

She then looked at the haze of Febreze billowing from the window.

"Thomas, what's going on?" she shouted again.

"Dog's shit in the living room again," he replied.

"Little bastard, I only went next door for five minutes for a cup of tea and a natter!" she cursed loudly.

She advanced towards the house. "God, it stinks," she said under her breath and as she moved closer to the house, she addressed her son again.

"Have you picked the dog shit up yet?"

"Yes, mam."

"Well, hurry up and get it chucked on the allotment before I come inside."

A minute passed.

"Have you done it yet?" she asked.

"Yes, mam."

"Where've you put it?"

"On't vegetables like we always do," he replied.

"Good lad," she said and began to move towards the front door.

But I was frozen to the spot, my eyes as wide as dinner plates with the shock of what I had just heard. Did she just say what I thought she'd said? On the vegetables? I felt an involuntary gag but it wasn't Febreze this time, it was thought of what Ibra had consumed from the vegetable plot. Just as the full horror of the truth dawned, Mrs Blakely stopped on the threshold of the house and turned towards me.

"Are you alright, love?" she asked, noticing my pallid face. I couldn't reply. "It's alright, love, the smell will go in a minute." I gulped, the bile flooding my mouth. "Now then," she said, "how can I thank you for what you've done for our Thomas?" She paused for effect. I took a tentative, shallow breath.

She continued, "Our Thomas tells me that you loved the veg we gave you last year."

My eyes were screwed shut, my breathing still shallow, and my stomach doing the full 360 like a washing machine on full spin. I didn't have the nerve to tell her I'd given them away.

"So you know what?" She paused again.

I gulped once more, involuntarily, doubling over in anticipation of the loss of control of my bodily functions.

"You're lucky we've had a good start to the summer," said Mrs Blakely suddenly changing tack but I didn't notice, I was doing all I could not to vomit. Mrs Blakely was blind to my distress as she was so caught up in her own thoughts. I didn't notice that she had straightened herself up and neither did I see that she was also folding her arms as she came to a decision. She then began to speak again as I gasped for air.

"So, what do you reckon," she said, pausing for effect, like a conference speaker waiting for the audience to stop applauding.

"So, what do you reckon," she repeated, pausing once more before winking conspiratorially at me.

"To a few punnets of our fresh strawberries to say thank you for getting our Thomas a proper job?"

"Thank you," I said weakly, wondering how I was going to tell Ibra his organic vegetables were more organic than he may have wished.

As much as I respect and admire Ibra and how important he was to the success of the Work Project, the truth is, I never did.